ACKNOWLEDGEMENTS:

The author would like to thank
Alvina Ling, Connie Hsu, Kristine Serio,
and Christian Bauer for reading this
manuscript repeatedly and selflessly.
I would also like to thank Steven Malk,
Lindsay Davis, Jennifer de la Fuente,
Cari Phillips, Becca Hannon,
Caitlin Berry, Mike Nesi, Julia Jarcho,
Henry Kyburg, Julie Scheina, Andy Ball,
Amanda Hong, Joe Monti, Kirk Benshoff,
Wilfred Santiago, and Della Herden.

A NOVEL BY **SEAN BEAUDOIN**
ILLUSTRATIONS BY **WILFRED SANTIAGO**

Fade to Blue

LITTLE, BROWN AND COMPANY

New York   Boston

Little, Brown, and Company

Hachette Book Group
237 Park Avenue, New York, NY 10017
Visit our website at www.lb-teens.com

Little, Brown and Company is a division
of Hachette Book Group, Inc.
The Little, Brown name and logo are trademarks
of Hachette Book Group, Inc.

The publisher is not responsible for websites (or their content) that
are not owned by the publisher.

First Paperback Edition: February 2011
First published in hardcover in August 2009 by Little, Brown and
Company

Library of Congress Cataloging-in-Publication Data

Beaudoin, Sean.
  Fade to Blue / by Sean Beaudoin. — 1st ed.
    p. cm.
  Summary: Eighteen-year-old Goth Sophie Blue, sensing that
something is awry in her small town, begins to piece together the
connections between her missing father, a scientific researcher at a
local laboratory, and her high school's basketball star, Kenny.
  ISBN 978-0-316-01417-5 (hc) / ISBN 978-0-316-01418-2 (pb)
  [1. Identity — Fiction.   2. Experiments — Fiction.   3. Computer
programs — Fiction.   4. High schools — Fiction.   5. Schools — Fiction.
6. Family problems — Fiction.   7. Missing persons — Fiction.   8. Science
fiction.]   I. Title.

  PZ7.B3805775Fad 2009
  [Fic] — dc22
                                        2008032823

10 9 8 7 6 5 4 3 2 1

RRD-C

Printed in the United States of America

CHAPTER NONE
SOPHIE BLUE

THE TOWN POOL, THE SNACK BAR,
THE DEEP END, THE BIRTHDAY GIRL

The place was packed. I was in a lounge chair, Herb lay sprawled on the crusty cement, and Lake was wheeled between us, adjusting her tire pressure with little *pfft, pfft* sounds. In the parking lot, minivans pulled up in rows, disgorging knock-knees and beach towels and sloshy coolers. The lifeguard repeatedly blew his whistle. Candy wrappers fluttered like moths. The water shimmered and the sun beamed and a breeze softly blew.

It was a perfect day.

Except something bad was coming.

I could smell it in the chlorine. I could see it in the piles of abandoned flip-flops and skids of egg salad. It was in every yell and every shove and every stubbed toe. It was right there, on the tip of my tongue, just beneath the surface.

Which makes a ton of sense.

I popped my second can of Diet Crank (triple the caffeine, four times the aspartame), which tended to give me a definite style: Early Impressionist Panic Attack. My pad was filled with shaky portraits and possible tattoos: Godzilla playing bass, Caligula drinking a latte, Conan the librarian.

"What're you drawing?" Lake asked.

I was sketching her father in big swirly lines. He had a mound of hair in the center of his chest and lines of lesser fluff running from his neck to his toes. It was doubly obvious because he wore a pinstripe Speedo.

"Herb's chest-fro and banana sling."

Lake laughed. "Maybe someone should take a gander at their own ensemble?"

I was wearing a black bikini. Black Wayfarers. Black cowboy hat. Black boots, unlaced, no socks, and a black sweatband on my left wrist. My look was sort of Dead Southern Rocker, mixed with a studied nonchalance. A maybe-Aaron-Agar-will-show-up-chalance.

"Aaron Agar is not coming," Lake said, lighting a cigarette. I waved at the smoke with a sketch of an unhappy lung. The lifeguard blew his whistle, *Hey you! Put that out!*

"So, Herb?"

Herb raised his head, peering at me above the rim of his aviator shades. His nose was covered in zinc, glasses carving a line in the white goop.

"Yes, ma'am?"

"You're a few days early, but I love my present."

Herb had baked me a big round birthday cookie and shoved a drippy candle into the center. It sat on a napkin next to my leather jacket.

"You pretty much only turn eighteen once," he said. He'd just lost his job. We came to the pool because it was free. "Was I going to spare any expense?"

I gave him a big thumbs-up. He gave me the double thumbs-up back.

Bryce Ballar ran past us, yelled, "Test tube!" and belly flopped into the shallow end, splashing annoyed moms and uncovered snacks. The lifeguard blew his whistle. Bryce Ballar gave the lifeguard the finger.

"Do you hear that?" I asked.

Lake sighed. "Don't listen to anything Bryce —"

"No," I said. "*That.*"

There was a faint whispery clanging, like the buzz coming from someone's headphones. *Gotothelabgotothelabgotothelab.*

I stood up on the deck chair to hear better.

"What are you doing?" Lake asked.

"No standing on the deck chair!" the lifeguard yelled.

I could see my brother on the other side of the pool, near the Dumpster. He was reading a comic book, cross-legged on a yellow towel that looked suspiciously like a washcloth.

Gotothelabgotothelagotothelab.

"Um, Sophie?" Lake said.

I got on my tiptoes and waved but O.S. ignored me, glasses two inches from the page. Behind him, an ice-cream truck was coming down the hill. It had bullhorns mounted on the roof. Bells clanged and clown music jangled.

"That's weird," I said, my elbow suddenly numb.

"Yeah, it is," Lake said. "Sit down."

The truck's windows were tinted black, *Snap O' Matic* painted across the hood. It didn't slow down as it entered the parking lot, front wheels jumping the curb, dragging shrubbery. Gears ground, causing a series of backfires. The truck slammed through a big sign that said *Thank You Fade Labs, Pool Construction Complete!* Ice cream flew everywhere. Popsicles left melty trails of red. Kirsty Wells picked at her toes. Kirsty Rogers smoothed her towel. Floaty toys popped and burst. I looked at Lake, who didn't move. I looked at Herb, who yawned and rolled onto his belly. The truck veered left, aiming straight for the Dumpster.

I jumped off the chair and ran across the wet tiles, *slap, slap, slap.*

Thirty feet.

I knocked over benches, scrambling between tables.

Ten feet.

I slid sideways, windmilling for balance, and stood in front of my brother.

Impact.

The frozen metal grill connected with my chest, vertical imprints seared into me like barcode.

I am so Goth, I'm roadkill.

CHAPTER ONE
SOPHIE AND
MR. PUGLISI

TARDY? I DON'T FEEL TARDY

Mr. Puglisi and I looked at each other for about twenty minutes. He had a big head and a big, square face. He smelled like cigars and had a nose like a veiny gourd. On the wall behind him was a poster of a sad-eyed basset hound wearing an orange clown wig. Underneath it said *Happiness Is Relatively Relative*. I was supposed to meet Mr. Puglisi every day after lunch.

"What's your first name?" I asked, pointing to his nameplate.

"Mister," he said.

He was wearing an old sweater. There was a hole in the shoulder that looked ripped on purpose, like he was the kind of guy who made a great omelet and would take you fishing to teach you about life in the way he knotted worms on his hook.

"So how's Sophie today?" he asked.

Sophie has bad dreams about her brother. Sophie's house keeps being broken into. Pretty much around the clock Sophie's scared shitless. Also, Sophie's stuck in a tiny office with Mr. Sweater while he keeps referring to her in the third person.

"Pretty great," I said.

Mr. Puglisi searched my eyes for sarcasm and found it. He shuffled his notes. "A year ago you put a rather abrupt halt to your athletic career. I understand you were part of the soccer team?"

It was amazing how long ago that seemed. Running up and down a field. Kicking a ball and yelling and sweating and having fun.

"Sad, but true."

"Any particulars spur your change of heart?"

"The uniforms were ugly."

"Ugly in what way?"

"Pink."

"I wonder," Mr. Puglisi said, clearly not wondering, "what you make of the events that transpired on your seventeenth birthday?"

"Is this going to take much longer?" I asked. "Miss Last says we're doing conjunctive verbs today."

Mr. Puglisi frowned. "You may think flippancy shields you from having to deal with your feelings, Sophie, but it doesn't. It pushes us further away."

"Us?"

"Tell me about the name Test Tube," he said.

It was like having a freezing shower turned on. It was like being slapped by your best friend, out of nowhere, for borrowing a pair of socks.

"Have you ever been run over by a truck, Mr. P?"

"Puglisi," he said, and popped open a can of Sour White. "Did you at least bring your assignment?"

Each meeting, I was supposed to hand in an essay. The essay was supposed to list the things I remembered about the day my father left. Or disappeared. Or whatever. I'd already told him I didn't remember anything. He thought if we broke the day into bite-size chunks, it would all come rushing back, a slo-mo revelation with strummy guitars. I slid the paper across his desk. He licked his lips, reading aloud.

The Day My Father Disappeared, Essay #1

My father pulled onto the highway ramp.
"You ready to show them who's best, Soph?"
I knocked my cleats together, unloosening old mud. We were on our way to a soccer game, the second of the season. The week before, I'd scored a goal.
"You're staying for the game, right?"
"Absolutely," my father said. He pulled a pager off his belt, which jingled and then buzzed. "The whole game."

When the game was over, my father wasn't in the stands. All the other girls were laughing and slapping five, Kirsty Beck drinking juice boxes and Kirsty Zorn massaging her shins.
I walked up to the car. The engine was ticking. My father was leaning against the door, looking at his pager. "Great game!" he said.
"Did you see my goal?"
"Oh, yeah," he said. "Amazing!"
I hadn't scored a goal. "Thanks."
"Hop in, kiddo," my father said. "We need to make a quick stop at the lab."

We parked behind White, Fade, Templeton, and Sour. My father buttoned and straightened his lab coat. His name tag read ALBERT in big block letters.

"Why don't you come in a minute? I've just got to get something from my desk."

"I'm in shorts," I said, pretending to sniff my armpit. "I'm all sweaty."

"C'mon, Soph," he said, his glasses reflecting an oval of sun onto my knee. The building was squat and dark. We walked past cubicles, with a million tubes and pipettes and beakers. Dad told me to sit in the waiting room. I picked an orange plastic chair from a row of orange plastic chairs. There were the world's boringest magazines fanned on the coffee table, like Genetics Today and Gene Splice Digest and European Vacuum Quarterly. My father knocked on a steel door. A woman's voice ushered him through. Their conversation was muffled, but I could make out the occasional word, like must, won't, ready, and code. Then trail, nurse, dream, loop, and begin. A loud voice came over the intercom.

"Officer Goethe? Officer Goethe, please report to the testing area."

Footsteps double-timed down the hallway. A man in a security uniform clomped into the waiting room. His name tag said GOETHE — SECURITY OPS. He was big and slope-shouldered. There was a gun on his belt and a chrome briefcase in his hand. He stood in the doorway, and then a woman in a nurse's uniform came out of the office. She was beyond old, ancient, fossilized. She was wearing a heavily starched skirt so white it hurt my eyes.

"Hi, honey. I'm The Nurse," she croaked. "Do you like ice cream?"

"Where's my father?"

"This won't take a sec."

"What won't?"

"Go ahead and hold out your arm for me."

I kicked my cleats against the bottom of the chair. Blades of dried grass helicoptered to the floor. The Nurse glanced at the officer. He tried on a fake smile, teeth lined with a high brown watermark, then grabbed my wrist. The Nurse held a syringe. I tried to pull away, but she jabbed it into the crook of my arm. The pain rolled up from my toes. It was like slipping into a frozen pond, shards of black ice cutting along my sides. I tried to breathe but couldn't. I tried to move but couldn't. After a long time, The Nurse pulled the needle out and replaced it in the chrome briefcase, spinning an elaborate lock.

"Everything seems worse than it really is," she said, her breath like dust. Then she leaned close, crumbs in the tiny hairs on her chin, whispering, "You're going to have beautiful dreams. Don't fight them. I'll see you soon, birthday girl."

I looked down at my arm, positive there'd be a gaping wound, but it was only a tiny red mark, which immediately began to itch. I slumped in the orange chair. A swirl of nausea rose in my stomach. I closed my eyes as a series of numbers began to flash,

from left to right, like a stock ticker. Ones
and zeros, zeros and ones, faster and faster
until they blurred into a long white line.

Mr. Puglisi harrumphed. It sounded like a big, tired animal that
spent a lot of time grinding roots with its molars. "So, that is an
interesting essay. Very interesting."

Hearing it out loud was weird, like it was someone else's story.
I felt bad for the girl and had to keep reminding myself it was me.

"You have quite an imagination," Mr. Puglisi said.

I opened my pad and started drawing Mr. Puglisi stuffing
himself into a blender.

"Am I to judge by your expression that you wish me to believe
this story is, in fact, an accurate representation of events?"

In the drawing, Mr. Puglisi added ice and fruit.

"Let's go that route then, shall we? This injection. Can you
show me the mark?"

I gave him a long look. Then pulled up my sleeve. There was a
sore in the crook of my elbow, ugly and red. His pen scratched
across the page. I knew it was something like *Self-inflicted*, or
Recommend immediate removal of all sharp objects.

"What's it say?"

Mr. Puglisi held up his pad. *Visual evidence of arm trauma.*

I nodded, surprised.

"Have you spoken to your mother about this?"

"No."

"Why not?"

It was a thirty-hour answer. It was a weekend symposium.

"Because I didn't think she'd believe me. The police didn't."

"The police?"

"After Dad, there were interviews and stuff. A detective. Missing person report, the cop all like, 'Office? Show me this office.
Needle? Show me this needle.' I could tell he thought, Here's a
girl collects paper clips. Here's a girl calls bomb threats in to the

supermarket. He goes, 'Here's my card, don't call me.' He goes, 'I'll get back to you if I hear anything, which I won't, so don't hold your breath.' Trish slept through most of it."

"Trish?"

"Mom."

"You refer to your mother by her first name?"

I did. She insisted. It was kind of like hanging around with your cool aunt who actually wasn't your aunt and really wasn't all that cool.

"There's not much logic in Trish-world," I said.

"For instance?"

"For instance, I'm not allowed to have a cell phone. Or drive. It's like we're Amish. Except we're not."

"Well, lots of parents don't . . ."

I stopped listening, his voice all, *Mwaw, mwaw, mwaw.* Sophie *mwaw* mom *mwaw* teens *mwaw* test-kit *mwaw* future *mwaw* electives *mwaw.*

He reached over and snatched the notebook from my hand.

"Hey!"

Next to the drawing of him pureeing himself, I'd written:

I'm so Goth, bats pick up my sonar.
I am so Goth, I sprinkle staples on my Special K.
I'm so Goth, I keep toenail clippings in a mason jar.
I am so Goth, my black sweatband wears a black sweatband.
I'm so Goth, when I get my period, I bleed tiny mascara'd guitar players.

Mr. Puglisi sighed and handed me a detention slip. "Keep it up," he said. "I have more time than you can possibly imagine."

The principal's office was empty. His secretary was this anorexic lady with flaky skin who was knitting and putting on makeup at the same time. She pointed to the punishment bench.

"Thanks. I forgot where it was."

She dialed up her lipstick and pointed at a poster on the wall. It was a picture of Einstein making a face and sticking out his tongue. Underneath it said *Sarcasm Is the Retreat of Small Minds.*

"The secretary last year had a poster with a kitten stuck in a tree," I told her, scratching my elbow. "It said *Hang On in There.*"

"I am not the last secretary," the new secretary said.

I sketched her knitting herself a new personality. I sketched a giant hammer crushing the school like a naughty walnut. I sketched my father, holding my hand, as we walked forever away from here.

CHAPTER TWO
KENNY FADE

BITE ME, FOR I AM FULL OF CREAMY NOUGAT

Kenny Fade took the ball from the ref and lobbed it to Aaron Agar, who everyone called Freckle. Freckle dribbled upcourt and passed it back. Kenny spun by his man like the guy was stapled to the floor and slammed it. The crowd jumped and howled. A group of girls in the bleachers sucked on Popsicles, screaming *K-E-N-N-Y*. By the time they'd reached the second *N*, most of the parents joined in as well. The gym was a rumbling cannon, BLAM-*BOM* BLAM-*BOM* BLAM! Dayna Daynes, head cheerleader, bounced in time, some parts bouncing more in time than others. Her long tan legs kicked and scissored and leaped. Kirsty Minor followed her lead, completing the routine: *"Go, Kenny, Fade's our man, if he can't do it, nobody can! Fade, Fade, Fade, FA-DAY!"* Kenny winked. Flashbulbs popped. He stole the ball, took three slow dribbles, and drained a rainbow three.

"Way to go, *Fade!*" Coach Dhushbak yelled, in his tight shirt and nylon sweatpants. "Keep 'em guessing!"

"Fa-day, Nice play! Fa-day, Hoo-ray! Fa-day, Hot-tay!"

In the locker room at halftime, one of the assistant coaches brought over cookies and cans of Sour White. Kenny popped one but could barely swallow. The soda tasted foul, a pig's tail of nausea curling through his stomach. He gagged and tossed the can at a trash barrel across the room, dead center.

"Three-pointer!" someone yelled. Everyone laughed. Coach Dhushbak heard it and tore out of his office. On the wall behind him was a poster of a football player helping an old woman and her groceries across the street. Underneath it said *Sports Don't Build Character, They Reveal It.*

"All right, ladies, listen good!" Coach Dhushbak yelled, kicking a few chairs before giving one of his three speeches: Injured Teammate, God and Country, or Mel Gibson Wearing Kilt. The team barely paid attention. Everyone knew the game was already locked. And even if it wasn't, they had Fade. Some miracle comeback? They had Fade. Meteor attack? They had Fade. What was there to worry about?

Only the numbers racing through my head, Kenny thought. *Only the dead raccoon in my stomach and the rotting mayo in my veins.*

In the hallway outside the locker room, Dan Sellers's mother reached over and slapped Kenny's butt. Then she tried to hand him a slip of paper with her phone number on it. Coach Dhushbak frowned, hustling the team back into the gym. At the end of the bench, Kenny put his hand on Dan Sellers's shoulder. "Hey, don't worry about it."

"I can't believe her," Dan Sellers said. "Okay, for one thing? My father's funeral was six months ago."

"I remember."

But did he remember? Kenny wasn't sure. He might have been there in a suit, head down, nodding with the eulogy. He might have sneezed because of the freshly cut grass. On the other hand, maybe he was never there at all. Kenny's brain felt like a gray sponge. If you squeezed it with two hands, a bunch of dirty water would come out. Sometimes when he blinked there were double exposures, scratchy film of someone else's vacation playing behind his eyes. Still, he felt bad for the Sellers kid. "Listen, you want to come by the house sometime and talk, you're always welcome."

Dan Sellers looked up and sniffed. "Really?"

"Sure thing," Kenny said, scratching his elbow.

Dan Sellers wiped snot with the back of his hand. "Wow, I —"

"Besides, if you're really feeling bad, check that out." Kenny pointed to the wheelchair chick, sitting by herself under the bleachers smoking. "Remember her? Back when she was hot?"

Dan Sellers nodded.

"There's always someone else got it harder, you know?"

The whistle tweeted and the crowd cheered. Kenny gave Dan Sellers's shoulder a little punch and ran onto the floor. By the end of the third quarter Upheare High was ahead by thirty-three and Freckle Agar was dribbling in circles, running out the clock. When Coach Dhushbak pulled Kenny from the game, the crowd stood and clapped in unison. Dayna, absurdly pneumatic, blew kisses like an Italian starlet boarding a cruise ship. Coach Dhushbak slapped Kenny five and the guys on the bench slapped him five and all the dads in the first row slapped him five. Kenny belched greenly before parking it between Freckle and Zac, his two best friends. He'd finished with thirty-nine points.

"Could have had sixty if you wanted," Freckle said, a wisp of stubble on his chin.

"It's just sound marketing," Zac said, his gelled hair standing straight up. "K-dog knows scouts like to see a team player. A man who shares the ball *and* scores? That's a man belongs in Division One. Or hell, maybe just straight pro."

"C'mon," Kenny said, unlacing his size thirteen Dikes. Zac had the same pair. Freckle had the same pair. "Don't be a renob."

Zac raised an eyebrow. "Renob?"

"Will you remember us?" Freckle asked, leaning over and pretending to fawn. "When your limo pulls up outside the LA clubs and Zac and I shuffle by for autographs? Will you at least let us touch your sweats?"

"Dude," Kenny said.

"*Dude,*" Zac said.

"Seriously, dude?" Freckle said. "How 'bout you front us a couple supermodels?"

"You asshats already got girlfriends."

"Not like Dayna, we don't," Zac said.

"It's Fade's world," Freckle agreed. "We just live in it."

Kenny sat back, scratching his elbow, which had gone numb. It could have been a good game if he hadn't spent it riding out waves of queasy foam.

"Hey, you look a little green there, Kenny," Freckle said, lowering his voice. "Maybe you should go see the nurse?"

CHAPTER THREE
SOPHIE BLUE

IT'S JUST LIKE A HORROR MOVIE, EXCEPT NO CAMERAS OR LIGHTS OR ACTORS, AND ALSO, IT GOES ON FOREVER

Ring. Ring. Ring.

Sophie (whispering): "Hello?"

Lake (whispering): "Hey, it's me."

Sophie: "Thank God, I was lying here so not sleeping. You wouldn't believe what . . ."

Lake (yawning): "Me, too. What's that noise?"

Sophie: "Trish's flat screen."

Lake: "They have game shows on at midnight?"

Sophie: "I guess there's lonely people in every time zone."

Lake: "It's true. Dad's downstairs reading *Siddhartha* or something."

Sophie: "Wouldn't it be funny if we hooked Herb and Trish up? Then we'd be half sisters. Or stepsisters."

Lake: "I don't, ah . . . I don't think Dad's quite ready for Trish."

Sophie: "Yeah. Even with a six-month crash course, he'd still —"

Trish (picking up the extension and breaking in): "What a surprise. And with school tomorrow. Say goodnight, ladies."

Lake: "Sorry, Miss Blue."

Trish: "Sorry, my dear, is in the ear of the beholder."

Click.

Lake (whispering): "What does that even mean?"

Sophie: "It means someone's dosage needs to be upped."

Lake (giggling): "G'night."
Sophie: "Wait, I —"
Click.

My room is on the third floor, in the attic. Trish's is in the middle, and O.S.'s is down in the dungeon. The house is an old Victorian, big and pointy, like Leather Face signed up for some design courses and drew it himself. After Dad left (kidnapped by opium cartel? spontaneously combusted?) we all sort of claimed our own floor. You can go days without seeing anyone. Hearing them is another matter. My brother's half-digested Hot Pocket, for instance, tends to boom up through the floorboards. Then there's the banging that comes from Trish's room: Put Upon (throwing one shoe) and More Put Upon (throwing two shoes).

Clonk, clonk.

The double stiletto is code for *Turn that stereo down, Sophie, I can't hear my show!* What it isn't code for is *Don't worry, hon, I understand your stereo is way up because my show is so ridiculously loud two-thirds of our neighbors know which contestant just won the keys to a brand-new Dodge Flatus.*

I lowered the CD, *Rosie and the Pussybats Live at Budokan,* and then tiptoed down the stairs. Trish was standing in the hallway with a cup of tea like she was trying to remember what she was there for.

"You went for a cup of tea."

She jumped a little, spilling some on the floor, then wiped it with her furry slipper.

"What are you doing down here?"

"I can't sleep."

"Do you have a headache?"

Headache was Trish code for period. "Sometimes girls get headaches," she'd told me the first time as I stood there horrified while she wadded up toilet paper in the bathroom stall of a restaurant. O.S. sat out in a booth by himself, chomping breadsticks for an hour.

"It's not that," I said. "I think the house was broken into again."

Someone kept punching in the downstairs windowpanes. We'd come home and find papers strewn, boxes upended, junk in my room tossed around. The police had concluded it was just local kids since nothing was ever stolen, but it kept happening.

Trish made her It's All Just Greek to Me face. "Anything else?"

I cleared my throat. "Well, there's this Popsicle truck. Outside my window. It makes noise all night."

Trish raised the pencil line where her eyebrow used to be. "Popsicles? Sophie, why didn't you say so? I'll dial the authorities first thing in the morning."

"Great," I said. "Thanks."

I walked downstairs, holding my nose. My brother was sitting in the kitchen. O.S. stands for Old Spice. It's been his name since he was six and found a bottle in Dad's drawer and poured it all over himself, a habit he still hasn't broken.

"Hey, O.S."

He looked up from his comic book, *Suck Me Twice,* issue twelve. Nude vampire chicks frolicked on the cover. There was also a copy of *Splickity Lit #4: Splickity Learns Farsi.* O.S. pushed his glasses up his nose and coughed. In front of him was an actual plate, instead of a clump of dirty napkins and Hostess wrappers. On the plate sat three stalks of celery.

"You on a diet?"

O.S. picked up a stalk and sniffed it. He made a face and rubbed his shaved head. "Oh, man, it's hard to explain. I've been having a new urge?"

"Puberty," I said. "Try saltpeter."

O.S. didn't laugh. The gut under his T-shirt looked like he was smuggling hams out of East Berlin. O.S. used to be skinny. He used to have hair. When Trish asked why he cut off all his beautiful curls, O.S. said, "Um, the ladies wouldn't stop running their fingers through them?"

I found a clean mug and dumped in three packets of cocoa powder. My brother held his celery out like a pointer. "Well?"

There was also a time, before Dad, that O.S. didn't phrase every single thing he ever said as a question.

"Well, what?"

"I know something bad is coming?"

I jumped. Literally straight up. "You do?"

"Yeah. I can tell by the look on your face, so you might as well spill it."

I leaned against the sink. Water began to wick along my back and down my skirt, but I didn't move.

"Have you, sort of, by any chance, been hearing weird noises?"

"Noises?" he said.

"Like, outside? Whispering, or jingling or static or whatever?"

"All I hear in the basement is the pipes whoosh every time you flush, which, unless you're destroying state's evidence, is way too often."

"Good one. Evidence."

"Thanks for coming," he said. "I'll be here all week."

"Seriously," I said. "I've been having dreams."

"Me, too."

"Really? Because —"

O.S. sucked in his gut. "Yeah, I keep having a sort of sci-fi one where I'm tall and muscular? But ironically, I now live on a planet where everyone's secret fantasy is to be a bald fat kid."

"Don't you hear that ice-cream truck jangling all night?"

He stopped smiling. "Ice-cream truck?"

"Outside. Waiting."

I could tell he was trying to decide whether I was sort of full of crap or really packed all the way to the rim. There was a click in the hallway that could have been Trish's door. O.S. put a finger to his lips.

"Listen," I whispered. "Something bad *is* coming. I can feel it."

"Maybe something bad has already come?" O.S. whispered back. "I mean, have you looked around here lately?"

"I know, but —"

"Maybe you should go see the nurse?"

"*What?*"

"You know? Like, tomorrow? At school?"

My mouth opened, but there was nothing there, not even a whisper. My brother wrapped up his comics and tiptoed down the stairs. The celery he left where it was.

I slipped back into my room and closed the door.

Ring. Ring. Ring.

Sophie: "Hello?"

Lake: "Hey, it's me."

Sophie: "Yeah, I figured."

Lake: "I forgot to tell you about your birthday present."

Sophie: "You're still early. Forty-eight more hours."

Lake: "I'm not early, I'm ramping up. First, there's the congratulatory call. That's what this is. Then I say it in person. That's tomorrow. Then the huge Styrofoam cake gets wheeled into class. A Styrofoam cake, which, incidentally, Aaron Agar jumps out of naked."

Sophie (inhaling too obviously): "Naked?"

Lake (sly giggle): "Well, no, not entirely."

Sophie (abject disappointment): "How not entirely?"

Lake (just the facts, ma'am): "He's wearing a bowtie. And freckles."

Sophie (an unhappy shopper who knows her rights): "That's *way* too much coverage."

Trish (picking up the extension and breaking in): "This is the very last time, ladies. Then we move into stage three."

Lake: "Totally *my* fault, Miss Blue."

Sophie: "Stage three? I thought we were in code yellow."

Trish: "I am not kidding. Why are you acting like I'm kidding?"

Click.

Sophie: "Listen, I need to tell you —"

Lake: "Anyway, I'll see you in PE."

Sophie: ". . . something —"

Click.

By midnight, my room was dark and silent and cold. My candles were all melted. It was too late for Lake to call again. O.S. was asleep. Even Trish's TV was quiet. It was just me. In the attic. With the ringing bell and the jangling clowns and the buzzing static.

Dong, dong, dong.

I shimmied out the window in the corner of my room, which was a tiny wooden oval with a broken latch. If I hooked my legs onto the trim, I could swing my body just enough to reach the eaves and lever myself over the lip of the roof. A long time ago, my father hammered a two-by-four into the shingles so you could brace your heels and lean back against the mansard and stare into the sky. The two-by-four was old and brown. The nails were rusty. Sooner or later it was going to come loose. I got a swervy feeling in my stomach thinking about it, so I made sure to think about it more. I could practically see the entire town. I spread my arms like wings.

"SO COME AND GET ME ALREADY!"

My voice echoed. A dog barked.

"THE POPSICLE MAN HAS A HOOK FOR A HAND! HE EATS BROKEN GLASS AND RUSTY TACKS AND STACKS OF LIGHTLY SEASONED ORPHANS!"

My voice faded away, carried by the wind, not even an echo this time. The Popsicle Man did not yell back.

Just because you're paranoid doesn't mean they're not still after you.

Jangle, jangle, jangle. Buzz buzz buzz.

CHAPTER FOUR
KENNY FADE

IT'S PRONOUNCED "FA-DAY"

Kenny Fade was the last one in the showers after the game. He stood with his head under the far spigot. Hot water coated his hair and face, running down his legs and into the large drain in the middle of the floor.

"Dude, stop staring at my junk!"

"Whatever, Mini Me, you can't stare through a microscope!"

Kenny scratched his elbow, the skin raw and sensitive, listening to the guys talking smack, how they stole a ball or blocked a shot, how they schooled their man or were slick under the basket with a pass.

"Mother of God, did you see the thong on Kirsty White?"

"All that ass? You could feed, like, two starving countries on that ass."

The stories were all the same, the inflections the same, the laughs the same.

"Move over, dirt merchant, I don't want you within a *yard* of my towel."

"You, my friend, are a total homo-sexer. I advise you to apply to college and major in fashion."

Eventually, someone would crank up the boom box and someone would toss talcum powder, and someone would run around in their jock fake-punching people and going: "Hey, *where* the party at? Hey, where the party *at*? Dude, where *is* the par-*tay* at?"

Kenny stayed in the shower with his eyes closed until there were no more lockers slamming, voices echoing farther and farther down the hall.

Across the room came an ugly metallic scrape.

Kenny figured it was Zac, dragging a chair to make some freshman stand on and sing the fight song, but when he looked over, there was no one there. Kenny turned off the tap and reached for his towel. Lockers popped and pinged, the aluminum cooling. On the far wall was a poster of a skinny kid with this colossal rash on his thighs. Underneath, it said *Make Hygiene Your Best Buddy.*

"Hello?"

The spigot at the other end of the room swiveled on. By itself.

"Zac?"

The room began to fill with steam. Kenny thought he heard a tiny whisper, like radio static. *Purse.* Or *Nurse.* Faint and then gone.

"Freckle?"

No answer.

"Coach?"

gotothelabgotothelab

Kenny walked over and shut off the tap. His elbow itched. He scratched at the scar, the size of a quarter, red and raised. His gym bag, which had been on the bench in front of his locker, was now on the floor, his stuff tossed like someone had rooted through it.

"Hey!"

The spigot on the opposite wall snapped on. Kenny jumped, literally straight up.

"Not funny." He turned the tap back off. "Ass-hats?"

Wind blew through the cement hallway. Kenny was ready to just grab an armload of clothes and run up the stairs naked, when all the showerheads came on at once. He yelped, retreating to the drain cover, the only place the jets didn't reach. The water was scalding. His toes burned as the water changed color, at first pink, then darker, Popsicle red. A big syrupy lip bled toward him, dark enough that he could see his reflection.

It almost looked like he was wearing a skirt.

CHAPTER FIVE
OLD SPICE BLUE

O.S. SPEAKS, YOU LISTEN

How PE works? The upper echelon, sport-oriented males and attractive females, sit on the bleachers near the windows. Those of us overweight or otherwise damaged, dingy, unwashed, cave-chested, stork-shaped, nonathletic, or generally female-resistant sit by the jockstrap barrels.

"It is always smelling like the ass," Karl-Heinz said, wrinkling his nose as sweaty Connors and sweaty Jeds zoomed by, passing, dribbling, yelling "Here, here, here. Dude, HERE!" A year ago, Karl-Heinz transferred from a school in Ohio. His real name is Marty. The first day, he pretended to speak almost no English. Teachers immediately forgave grammar mistakes, didn't demand homework, and took his complete lack of interest to be a sign of cross-cultural incomprehension. Even Coach Dhushbak leaves him alone.

"Um, you could try holding your breath?" I suggested.

"Ya, ya," he said.

I unwrapped a Nut-Buddy Mallo-Cake as my sister and Lake came through the doors at the other end of the gym. They picked their own empty row, just like us, but were somehow able to project a face-saving intent. Sophie slipped off her leather jacket, revealing a cutoff band shirt that said Doktah Jack and the Kevorkians. Pretty much every guy in the gym stared. Even Karl-Heinz eyed her clinically.

"Is hard to belief you are twins, ya?"

At this point he was unable to completely turn off the accent. His parents had already taken him to three doctors, who all prescribed Ritalin. He was gobbling about six hundred milligrams a day.

"Seriously, with the twins thing?" I said. "Oh, man, that's some hilarious material."

He shrugged. On the wall above him was a poster with an enormously fat kid surrounded by laughing jocks. Underneath it said *The Four Major Food Groups: Fries, Fries, Shakes, and Fries.*

"What do you think of the girl she's with?" I asked.

"I belief that chick is in a wheelchair, ya?"

"Yes," I said. "She is."

Bryce Ballar ran by with two bottles of talcum, tossing it in the air. "It's snowing!" he laughed. Karl-Heinz swore in German. Powder speckled my issue of *The Adventures of Destruktor-Bot and Manny Solo, Boy Mentor,* reducing it from mint-minus to very good/very good-plus. Would Destruktor-Bot have accepted the insult so easily? Ah, no. While Destruktor-Bot wanted nothing more than to shed a real human tear, a lot of the time he just sort of redlined and smashed shit up. I definitely wanted to redline and smash shit up, too. I was, however, unequipped with a massive titanium fist.

"O.S.?" Karl-Heinz said, pointing across the gym.

"Yeah?"

"Your sister, she is waving to you."

"She is?"

"Go and say the hello, the how are you. Talk like a man to your new girlfriend."

"Hoo, boy," I said, mentally willing my breath to smell better.

"Hey, O.S.," Lake said. On her lap was a book, *Venkman's Astoundingly Unusual Words and How to Use Them, Vol. II.* I tried to think of something to say about it and failed. Her hair was blond and messy. She wore a rumpled shirt and jeans. There was a tiny, lovable gap between her front teeth. Her eyes were speckled green. And they were waiting for me to say something.

I came up with *Hi!*

Coach Dhushbak blew his whistle three times. "Get over here, Blue!"

Sophie trudged onto the court. She refused to wear the Upheare Toros purple shirt and shorts. Coach Dhushbak gave her a speech heavy on the word *mandatory*.

"Don't you just love gym?" Lake asked.

"Watching Sophie play volleyball in fishnets and combat boots? It almost makes it worth it."

Lake laughed. It was little and sparkly, the kind of laugh you'd make up just about any dumb joke to hear again. I couldn't think of a single dumb joke. Not even a knock-knock. My knees started to sweat. I looked at her arms, the little blond hairs that rose softly from them, and had to force myself to look away. After her accident, people kept saying, "What a shame, she had so much going for her." What they really meant was: *That could (and probably should) have happened to someone a whole lot less popular.*

"We're not the only ones who think so," Lake said, pointing.

On the other side of the court, Jed and Connor and Liam and Ralph were standing in a group, trying to decide if Sophie was scary hot. Or just scary. Did they believe the Rumor? Was Test Tube true?

"Bet you ten dollars she gets another detention," Lake said as Coach Dhushbak handed the slip over. While on his tiptoes. One time, Bryce Ballar goes, *Um, excuse me, Coach, but are there some X's and O's you need to diagram down Gothika's shirt?* Everyone laughed. Bryce Ballar got detention for a month.

The Rumor began right after Dad left. No one remembers who started it. That's the thing about a rumor, you can let it go like a bird, and instead of looking at your hands, people watch it fly away. Sophie heard it but didn't laugh. She traded the soccer shorts for a tube of Midnight Noir lipstick instead.

Sophie folded the detention slip into an origami swan, dropped it on the floor, and sat back down. "Dhushbak is a renob," she said, pulling out her pad.

Lake looked *renob* up in *Venkman,* but there was nothing between *renaissance* and *renal calculi.*

"Is that rooted in the Latin?"

Sophie didn't answer, pretending not to stare at Aaron Agar.

"Stop staring at Aaron Agar," Lake said.

Sophie drew a skeleton wheeling Lake into the pool.

"So stare already," Lake said. "But at least go ask him for his phone number."

Sophie drew Lake floating. Crocodiles with gaping jaws and hypodermic teeth closed in.

"Fine," Lake said. "But if you wait, some low-cut Kirsty is going to snap him up."

The Rumor was that Dad did something. To Sophie. Bringing home equipment from the lab. Bringing home test tubes. Being a pervert. Sophie having to go to the hospital. Dad having to leave town after the police found out. Once Sophie went Midnight Noir, though, it pretty much went underground. Ripped black tights mean *maybe that crazy chick has an Anarchy tattoo and a blog about bomb schematics.* Big black boots mean *maybe Gothika's got a list of who she's going to shoot first. And then second. And then third.*

The volleyball game got louder. Jeds jumped, Connors fell. Sophie stopped drawing. She was writing on her yellow pad, but now it was just lines of numbers, 00010101001010101010101 010000001.

"What's that supposed to be?" Lake asked.

"I dunno. It's sort of like counting sheep."

"It's binary code," I said.

"Bi what?"

"It's a computer language. Like, how computers talk to each other?"

"What are you counting sheep for?" Lake asked.

"I dreamed I was run over by an ice-cream truck last night," Sophie said.

"That's messed up," Lake said.

"Yeah," Sophie said, pulling up her shirt. There were big purple bruises in vertical lines across her ribs. "Especially since, in the dream, the truck hit me right here."

Jed and Connor and Liam and Ralph stared. Dieter, Samuel, Constantine, Prajit, and Wally stared. Karl-Heinz stared. Sophie pulled her shirt back down and scratched her elbow so hard it bled. Red drops plopped onto the floor in threes.

"Maybe you were lying on a book?" I guessed.

"Yeah, maybe," Sophie said. "But then what's that?"

Through the dirty window on the other side of the gym, I could just make out a mean-looking truck, jacked up, with tinted windows, idling in the parking lot. It could have sold Popsicles. It also could have been delivering spinach to the cafeteria or barrels of pomade to Coach Dhushbak. Lake wheeled over to get a better look. The truck backfired, interrupting Aaron Agar's serve. The ball banged off the net, coming to rest near Sophie's boot. He waited for her to grab the ball and toss it back. She didn't. No one said a word. Not Dieter, Samuel, Constantine, Prajit, or Wally. Not Jed or Mike or Connor or Bradley or Ralph. Eventually, Kirsty Swann went back to the office to ask Coach Dhushbak for a new ball. When I looked up again, the truck was gone.

"Do not pass go," Lake said. "Do not pass Goth. Chapter One: How to Make Friends and Influence Classmates."

Sophie made a face and palmed the volleyball. Aaron Agar held out his hand. Instead of throwing it to him, she launched it at the basket at the other end of the court. It flew over everyone's head in a crazy arc, spinning backward, hanging in the air. It was like a diorama of the three wise men, all of us staring at the little felt North Star. The ball swished through the hoop. *Snap.* The whole gym started yelling, going crazy. Coach Dhushbak burst out of his office, blowing his whistle. *What? What? WHAT?*

Sophie sat down and drew Dracula sipping a martini, three onions, an extra olive, and, at the end of the toothpick, a little bloody heart.

CHAPTER SIX
KENNY FADE

TRUCK WITH TINTED WINDOWS TO WHICH
NO KIDS WOULD EVER COME RUNNING,
NO JANGLING QUARTERS OR APRONED
HOUSEWIVES OR STICKY LITTLE FUDGESICLE HANDS

The next morning, there was a space for Kenny's Jeep in the student lot, right up front. No one ever said anything, but it was known to be his, always empty so he didn't have to walk an extra twenty feet to the door. Dayna met Kenny at his locker, her timing uncanny. She grabbed his butt and planted one on him.

"What's up, player?" Zac asked, leaning against Kenny's locker, which had been pried open. All his junk was tossed around. *Fade Rules* was now spray-painted across the front.

"Listen, guys," Kenny said, closing the door. "I need to tell you something."

"You're pregnant," Freckle said, playing with the drawstring of his hoodie.

"You're queer," Zac said, his blond hair shellacked straight out. He had on a designer shirt with the collar up, and expensive yellow goggles perched on his forehead.

"No, seriously. Something happened in the shower room last night."

"Did I guess it?" Zac said, holding his arms up like he'd won the lottery.

Kenny sighed. "Great. Thanks for listening."

The bell rang. Miss Last looked Kenny up and down while he found his seat, and then began explaining conjunctive verbs.

"Ahem . . . Mr. Fade? Could you come to the board and diagram this sentence for us?"

Kenny shuffled to the front and didn't even look at the sentence, writing words randomly, adding unnecessary letters, tossing in punctuation. Miss Last took the chalk, her hand lingering on his.

"Thank you, Mr. Fade, that is completely correct."

"No, it's not," Kenny said. "It's wrong."

"*Thank you, Mr. Fade,*" Dayna repeated from her desk, in a deeper, sexier voice. "That is totally, completely, *deeply* correct."

Everyone laughed. Kenny sat back down and wrote Dayna a note. *I need to talk to you. It's serious. Something happened last night.* Dayna took the note, wrote something, and handed it back. *I love you, too.* Kenny turned it over and scribbled furiously. *Did you read what I wrote? I think something's really wrong.* Dayna handed it back. There were no words at all this time, just a lipstick imprint and a smiley face. Kenny crumpled the note and threw it on the floor. Finally, the bell rang. Miss Last gave Kenny a wink as he merged into the flow of hallway traffic, a full head and shoulders above a stream of heads and shoulders. He took a left by The Nurse's office, nearly walking into a knot of boys who'd formed a circle around a fat kid with a shaved head. One of the boys knocked the kid's books to the floor.

Kenny pushed his way into the center of the circle. "Leave him alone."

Bryce Ballar wheeled, fists up. He wore a thick layer of fat like a winter coat, wide and solid underneath. Kenny was sure Bryce was going to kick his ass, but when Bryce saw who it was, he tried out a smile, teeth craggy with chocolate.

"Hey, K-dog."

"Hi," Kenny said.

Bryce signaled his underlings, who let the bald kid go. "Nice game on Friday," he said, melting back into the crowd.

Kenny's shiny red Jeep cornered hard out of the parking lot, the engine growling like a Rottweiler dying to be let off its leash. Dayna leaned forward in the passenger seat, applying a coat of orange gloss to her already orange lips. Sheriff Goethe drove by and gave a friendly honk. Cars of teenagers sped past in all directions, giddy about leaving school, blaring music, everyone flashing lights or yelling *KENNY!* out the window.

"Stop scratching," Dayna said. Kenny stared at his bloody fingernails. His elbow was red and raw. Dayna opened the glove compartment, shuffling through papers and gum wrappers and change.

"What're you looking for?"

She shrugged and went back to her lips.

"So have you heard any gossip or whatever about a lab?" he asked. "Like someplace in town, maybe?"

Dayna winked at him. "There something you need to get tested for?"

"Yeah, right," Kenny said, flushing. "No, it's just, some of the guys have been talking about this place. It's supposed to be . . . cool."

Dayna frowned, finishing her Sour White and tossing the can over her shoulder. The wind whipped it away, bouncing in the rearview until a truck creamed it flat. Dayna undid her belt and stood between the roll bars as another car pulled alongside. It was Bryce Ballar's convertible, fishtailing in gravel, half on the shoulder. Kenny honked, signaling for Ballar to fall back. They raced in tandem, blocking both lanes.

"Move over!" Kenny yelled.

"Whoo!" Bryce Ballar yelled.

The two cars roared down a straightaway and over a hill. On the horizon, an ice-cream truck sped toward them. Its rusty grill was mean-looking and low to the ground. The windows were tinted and a bullhorn mounted to the roof blared chanting music. The truck accelerated on the next straightaway, straddling the yellow line. Kenny slammed on the brakes, swerved, just missing Ballar's rear quarter-panel. The ice-cream truck back-fired, a long strip of flame shooting from its tailpipe, and shot past, racing away.

"God, did you see that?" Kenny asked. "It was like it was trying to . . ."

"Bryce is crazy." Dayna laughed, sitting back down and patting her hair. "Don't you think?"

"Totally insane," Kenny said, edging back into traffic.

"Don't worry, it's not like I think he's cute."

"I wasn't worried."

Dayna took Kenny's hand and stuck his entire index finger in her mouth. He flicked the turn signal. "I think we should go down by the docks and ask around. Maybe check out this lab."

"Let's just go to your house," Dayna whispered huskily, digging her Popsicle-red nails into his thigh. "And check out your room instead."

The front door was open. Kenny's mother, Rose, sat on a white leather couch that angled away from an enormous stone fireplace. She was knitting a white sweater. Or maybe it was a white vest, since there were no arms.

"Rock and roll!" she said, getting up and giving Kenny a hug. "The football hero!"

"Basketball," Kenny said.

Rose put out a plate of cookies. She was tall and blond and severe, her skin as pulled and tucked as the tight white dress that hugged her waist. She had a way of smiling that was hungry and bored at the same time. Zac and Freckle thought she was hot.

Dayna air-kissed Rose. The dog, a little shaggy mutt, came over and licked Kenny's hand. The mutt didn't have a name.

When they'd gotten it, Rose insisted on calling her Dog. She was like, "Well, it's a dog, right?"

Dog wagged her tail, which had a red ribbon tied to the end. There was a little black circle on her tummy that Kenny traced with his finger.

"Want a smoke?" Rose asked, lighting one for herself.

"No, thanks."

Rose pulled a cooler from behind the sofa. "How about a brewski?"

"No."

"*No?*"

"It's midseason," Kenny said. "I'm in training."

"Oh, right," Rose said. "Commitment. Teamwork. Keep it up."

Dayna accepted a beer and took a big swig. The television in the background flickered, some hospital show where all the doctors were ridiculously handsome, ethical, and really, really wanted to help lower-income patients get better.

"So," Rose said, winking at Kenny. "What are you guys up to tonight?"

"Nothing," Kenny said.

Dayna smiled coyly, squeezing Kenny's arm.

Rose laughed. "Hey, say no more. I guess I'll get out of your way."

"You're leaving?" Kenny asked.

"Sure, why not? I need something from the hardware store."

"The hardware store's closed."

"I need something from the yarn store," Rose said. A button popped off her blouse and rolled under the couch. Dog got up and sniffed it.

"There *is* no yarn store," Kenny told her.

"Then I'll walk over to the clinic," Rose said, patting her flat stomach. "Your mother needs the exercise."

"Ha!" Dayna laughed, giving Rose a high five before the door closed behind her. Dog turned three times in front of the fireplace and lay down. Dayna got on her knees in front of Kenny and slowly unlaced and removed his Dikes. She peered in each, as if looking for a treasure, and then put them carefully beside the door. Then she went to the multi-multi-buttoned stereo and chose some uncomplicated jazz. She took Kenny by the hand and started kissing his wrist, slowly working her way up until their mouths locked. Kenny took off his shirt, stomach corded into an anticipatory knot. Dayna took her shirt off as well, showing the handiwork of a benevolent god. Kenny knew if Freckle or Zac could see him now, they'd be punching each other on the arm and talking about how insanely stacked she was, how he was the luckiest guy in the world. He didn't feel lucky. He felt like he was drowning, and began to imagine himself picking up her clothes from the pile on the floor. And putting them on. Sliding into the dress and rolling up the pantyhose. Maybe even putting on some of her lipstick.

What the hell?

Kenny shoved Dayna off the couch and ran down the hallway, locking himself in the bathroom. He turned the faucet all the way up, refusing to answer Dayna's knocking. She called and pleaded. She banged and kicked. She begged him to open up, but he wouldn't answer, and she finally went home.

CHAPTER SEVEN
POPSICLE MAN 1.0

0000101010001010

1 110010100001010100000010101010100100101010100100100101010000010101010110100100100000101010100100101011110101101101101010000100010010010101000001010100100101010101010101010000010101111101100110110010000100100101011111110101010101010001010101001001001001010101010101010101010101010101.

Ignition.

CHAPTER EIGHT
SOPHIE AND
MR. PUGLISI

THE DAY MY FATHER DISAPPEARED, ESSAY #2

I slid it across the desk and Mr. Puglisi read it out loud.

Officer Goethe was holding my arm, trying to pull me up. The nurse was gone. I was half conscious. I had something tucked under my arm. It was a magazine, thin and glossy, with pictures of a robot. It fell to the floor. My father grabbed it, pushed the officer away, and scooped me into his arms. He hurried out into the parking lot, laying me in the backseat. I woke up halfway home, dazed. My father pulled over and ran into a store for an ice cream pulling the wrapper off with his teeth as he maneuvered through traffic. "Here, honey, this will get you going." I didn't want the ice cream but held it as it began to melt down my fingers and pool on the floor mat. I set the stick in the center of the mess.

"You okay, Soph?" he asked.

"I am okay," I answered. It was like my voice was coming from outside of me.

"In a year, you'll be eighteen," he kept saying.

*　　*　　*

In the kitchen, Trish was rewarming dinner. "You're late. Where were you?"

I stumbled past her, sick, too tired to explain. Halfway up the stairs, my mother and father were already arguing. Something slammed. I stood in front of my room, hand on the doorknob, and then went down to Old Spice's. The light was off.

"Hey, are you awake?"

O.S. sat up and yawned.

"Sort of."

I stood in front of the bed. Ugly words came through the floorboards. "Why don't you bring her a dozen roses?" Trish yelled. "With an elderly woman? What are you, sick?"

"She did it!" he kept saying. "It came back with her! Do you understand what that means?"

Doors slammed. A bottle broke.

"Are you okay?" O.S. asked.

I nodded, fingers massaging my forearm where the injection had gone in. There was a bump that ached and itched at the same time.

"Move over."

I climbed onto the bed, knocking a stack of comics to the floor. We curled up together, something we hadn't done since we were little.

"Remember when we used to take our blankets and pillows and sleep in the bathtub?"

"Yeah, I remember," he said sleepily. "You used to make me lie at the drain end. The water dripped on my forehead all night."

"Yeah, sorry about that," I said.

O.S. giggled and then got quiet. In a while, he started to snore. I pulled the blanket around him tighter and, as I did, noticed his elbow. Just beneath the cuff of his pajamas he had a scar, a small red bump in the exact same spot as mine.

"You think your brother had this . . . happen to him as well?"

"I don't know," I said. "I just remembered it."

"There's more here. Should I keep reading?"

"It's not from that day."

"This is before you went to the lab?"

I nodded. "It's the week before. I know I was only supposed to write about that day, but I thought . . ."

"It's okay, Sophie," Mr. Puglisi said. "You did the right thing."

"Maybe not," I said, and he started to read again.

My dog, Twinkle, was sick. She wouldn't run or play or eat. She wouldn't chase a ball. Twinkle just lay on her side and looked up with wet yellow eyes. Even when she saw me, her tail barely moved. I begged my father to bring Twinkle to the vet. He kept saying "If Twinkle's not better by tomorrow, we'll go."

The next day, I came home earlier than usual. I slammed my books on the counter and opened the door to the pantry. Twinkle was lying on her side, the black circle on her belly moving shallowly with her breath. She stared at my sneaker while my father injected something into her leg.

I stood with my mouth open. My father looked up.

"I'm giving her medicine."

"Did the vet say it will it make her better?"

"I hope so, honey."

A few hours later, Twinkle died. My father held my hand, and we had a ceremony, burying Twinkle in the backyard. I wanted to look in the box one last time, to say goodbye, but my father wouldn't let me. "You'll just get upset."

That night I tiptoed downstairs, knowing my father was going to the lab first thing. I wanted to get my soccer gear from the trunk. The car smelled funny. None of my gear was in there, but the trunk was full. Next to a bunch of lab equipment was a heavy black plastic bag labeled Sample #12 — Canis Control Group.

Mr. Puglisi paled. He cleared his throat while I stared at the new poster on his wall. It was a picture of a shy little Depression-era boy holding out a single rose. Underneath it said *I Wuv You.*

"Why don't we play a little game," he said. "You want to?"

I pictured us playing Twister. I pictured us playing Scrabble. I pictured us playing Texas Hold 'Em.

"Not so much."

"Let's do it anyway." He coughed and got his pencil ready. "I'm going to ask you a question, and I want you to answer the first thing that comes to mind."

"Like Rorschach without the blots."

"Correct," he said. "No blots. So what are you thinking right now?"

"I'm thinking about how excellent it would be if I had a pet rat named Boris."

He wrote it down. "What are you thinking about now?"

"I'm thinking about how excellent it would be if I had a thousand-gallon aquarium filled with doubloons and mermen."

He wrote it down. "What are you thinking about now?"

"I'm thinking about how excellent it would be if I had a giant drill-car that could bore its way to the center of the earth."

He took note after note, scratching away.

"Who do you think The Nurse is, really?"

"I have no idea."

"A representation of your mother, perhaps?"

"Representation?"

"Injections, needles, sharp objects," he said, "are all very common symbols."

"Symbols for what?"

He took a long time to clear his throat.

"I think you should return to this lab. Like, maybe today."

I tried not to shiver. And then did. "Why?"

"To look around. To have some closure."

"They don't even use *closure* in Renée Zellweger movies anymore. It doesn't mean anything."

Mr. Puglisi church-steepled his fingers under his chin. "We need to find out what happened to your father, Sophie. That's the first step toward a resolution."

"How? I can't just flip a magic switch and make it happen."

"That's what I'm here for, Sophie," Mr. Puglisi said. "So that we can find that switch and flip it together."

I considered the possibility that what he just said wasn't complete horseshit. The odds were poor. I held up his last detention slip. "Okay, since we're on the same team and all, do I still have to go?"

"You still have to go."

CHAPTER NINE
SOPHIE BLUE

WELCOME TO THE TIKI LOUNGE

I walked from Mr. Puglisi's office to detention down in the old science room. The door was closed, but Coach Dhushbak waved me in, one eye over the edge of his magazine, pretending not to stare. I sat in back. Coach Dhushbak blew his whistle, a quick chirp, and pointed to the desk closest to him. I rolled my eyes and got up and took a seat in the first row, but not the one he'd pointed to. There was a poster behind him of this clean-cut kid who was supposed to look like a troublemaker, with a boom box and a wallet chain and skateboard. Underneath it said *If Jimmy Had a Brain, He'd Be Dangerous.*

Coach Dhushbak twee'd his whistle. "No staring at the poster."

I pulled out my notebook and drew Coach Dhushbak stuffing himself into a wheat thresher. Chunky coach-parts came flying out the back, helping fertilize crops. Bryce Ballar sat on the other side of the room. He said something under his breath that sounded a whole lot like "rest rube."

"Quiet," Coach Dhushbak snapped.

"But, Coach, I totally saw Gothika staring at my junk!"

"Shut it, Ballar."

Bryce Ballar winked, showing his gums, which were impacted with cookie dough. The acne on his forehead was red and angry-looking.

"Hey, Coach, can you turn down the heat?"

"The heat's not on, Ballar, but it will be if one more word squeaks out your cakehole."

"*What a tool!*" Bryce said into his palm, pretending it was a cough.

"What's that, Ballar?"

"Nothin' Coach. Scratchy throat."

It was unbearably hot. A fly strafed the middle desks, making pass after pass. The sound of teachers locking up their classrooms echoed down the hallway. A tall janitor with orangey hair peeked in, frowned, and disappeared.

I looked at the clock. It was four fifteen. I drew a clown juggling skulls. When I looked at the clock again, it was four ten. I made the skulls on fire. Then it was four on the dot. The clock was moving backward. I looked again and the clock had no numbers. Where the twelve had been, it just said *Now*. Same with the three, five, and seven. *Now, now, now.* I blinked. Everything was like a bad video, shaky and Zapruderish. There was a low, insistent buzz. I looked at Coach Dhushbak, but he was locked in place. The page of his magazine was suspended midflip. His can of Sour White was half knocked over, the fizzy liquid sticking out in a little frozen wave.

Bryce Ballar was frozen, too, his mouth wide open. A piece of gum hovered between his teeth. I stood and snapped my fingers in front of him. Nothing. I leaned over, just an inch from his ham-hock face. Even with no breath, his breath stank. I flicked his gum with my pinkie. It rolled away, across the floor, but his mouth stayed open.

There was a tap.

On my shoulder.

I collapsed like an ironing board, just managing to grab the corner of the desk.

She was in a white uniform. In white shoes and white stockings. In a tiny white skirt. I knew it was her, even though she was totally different. She was hot. She was a sex bomb, with long blond hair and curve after curve after curve.

The Nurse was standing on a desk, with a perfect icy smile, one hand on her hip, the other holding a dog. Petting it. It was my dog. Twinkle. I could see the black circle on her belly that I used to trace with my finger.

The Nurse's body blinked, like a television getting bad reception. In. Out. In. She opened her mouth, but there was no sound. Twinkle yipped. The Nurse pointed to her watch. *Your birthday.*

"What?"

She made a sound, a tiny wheeze of static, like exhaling dust. She reached out, as if turning a dial.

"Happy birthday!" she said, clearer. There was huge white cake in front of her, with candles burning.

"How are you even here?"

"I'm The Nurse," she said, pointing to a badge on her white cloak that said ROSE FADE, NURSE ON DUTY.

"Rose Fade?"

"It's pronounced Fa-Day," she said. "What, you don't re-member?"

I was about to answer, but Rose Fade held up her hand. For a second she wavered, bad reception, her teeth no longer blindingly white. They were actually kind of brown. The same color as her eyes, which were dark and angry.

"We know now what you brought back out."

"Brought out of where?"

"They all thought it would be a device. All the techs said it was probably something electronic."

"Device?"

"We've been through your house a dozen times. It must be here, it must be there. But you were clever. Hiding the code in drawings. Very clever."

"What are you talking about?"

Rose Fade held up three fingers, lowering them one at a time.

"One, all roads lead to the lab. Two, O.S. does not stand for Old Spice." She lowered the last finger, which left the middle one pointing at me.

"Three, I want my picture book."

"What picture book?"

Her lip curled into a sneer. "The one your father stole. *La Nutrika*."

I looked back at the desk where my drawings sat. "You mean my sketch pad?"

"Tomorrow you'll be eighteen," she said. "Ignition. Come to the lab with *La Nutrika*, and as a birthday present I'll tell you what happened to Albert."

My entire body hummed. The hard part of being terrified, I thought, was what you did with the fear afterward. Who you were afterward. *I am different now.* Sophie Mach II. I have officially had a discussion with someone who's not really there. It was a whole new line to cross. This wasn't ride-your-ten-speed-down-a-flight-of-stairs crazy. It wasn't jump-out-of-a-plane-dressed-as-Elvis crazy. This was electroshock and oatmeal. This was meds under the tongue and plastic pee-pants and bored orderlies. And I was pretty sure there was no going back.

"I already know what happened to my father," I said, bluffing.

"Is that right?"

"He was killed by the Popsicle Man."

Rose Fade laughed. She leaned back and let out a dry wheeze, dust rising from her throat. "That's not possible."

"Why not?"

"Because your father *is* the Popsicle Man."

Numbers rushed into my head, thousands of them, in long chains, like water being forced into my ears, swirling around. I held my temples, pressing down, suddenly completely nauseated.

"I can't . . . he can't . . ."

Rose started to fade. In. Out. In.

"Welcome back to the Virtuality."

I squeezed my head harder.

Out. In. Out.

Out. Out. Out.

She was gone.

The buzzing sound stopped. Bryce Ballar's mouth crashed shut. "Ouch! Shit!" he yelled, holding his jaw, testing his front teeth. Coach Dhushbak's neck snapped back. His whistle got stuck mid-twee. He saw me in the middle of the aisle. "What in Christ, Gothika?"

His magazine page was still standing at attention. I watched as it slowly began to bend and fall. I watched as his soda became liquid and spilled across the magazine and into his lap.

"Standing without permission!" Coach Dhushbak said, slapping at the wet spot on his pants. He handed me a new detention slip.

"Great," I said gulping for air. "Thanks."

"One day you *will* thank me," he said. "One day, when . . ."

There was a sound outside, a backfiring, like a series of gunshots. An engine whined like it was about to explode. Bryce Ballar and Coach Dhushbak went to the window to see.

"Hey, Columbine-a, you got a quarter?" Bryce Ballar started to say. "I want to buy a chocolate —"

The Popsicle truck came smashing through the window frame, shattering glass. The massive engine barreled over desks and chairs, whining and growling and drooling.

"Daddy?"

The truck slid sideways, revving its engine. The clown music came on with a jangling that sounded like laughter. There was a high-pitched whine as its wheels spun in a patch of burning rubber, before it released the brake and crushed me against the chalkboard.

CHAPTER TEN
SOPHIE AND LAKE

AS YOUR LEGGY SCANDINAVIAN MODEL
PERSONA BUBBLES TO THE SURFACE

Sophie: "Oh, my God, you have to come over."

Lake: "Why, what's wrong? What's going on?"

Sophie: "What's going on? What is . . . I just . . . you wouldn't believe —"

Lake: "Okay, calm down. Take a —"

Sophie: "I'm not kidding, Lake. Get Herb out of bed. I feel like I'm about to lose —"

Lake: "But I can't just —"

Sophie: "Yes, you *can*."

Lake (after a long pause): "What about Trish?"

Sophie: "What about her?"

Lake: "Okay, okay, relax, I'll be there soon."

Click.

I guzzled two Diet Cranks, and they actually calmed me. I took deep breaths until I felt light-headed, then I did a drawing of Sasquatch, eating a hoagie. The Popsicle truck hadn't squealed around the corner for at least an hour. Or had it? No. Okay. It must have gone on break. He must have slammed the brakes. It was Dad? No way. It had to be a trick. The Nurse was a trick. The Nurse was a tick. I almost laughed, pacing between my bed and the wall.

It couldn't be him. I needed to not think. I needed to think of something else. Was that a sound? Was that jangling outside? I drew a guy with perfect teeth holding an armload of different toothpaste tubes. Underneath I wrote *Advertising: It Helps Me Decide.* I wondered if it was funny. I tore up the drawing. I wondered why there wasn't a short word for freezer, like *fridge. Reezer? Frez?*

You're losing it you're losing it you're losing it.

I jumped up and down for ten minutes, until Trish started tossing shoes.

I lay down with a pillow over my head. I flipped onto my left side and then my right.

What's taking Lake so long?

I thought about how she handled everything so much better than I did. Especially since fifteen minutes ago she was this fluffy blond cheerleader every guy in school was all trembly about and every girl was maxing mom's Visa to be just like.

"Oh, Lake, do you want to come out with Conner, Brad, and Tim for sushi?"

"Oh, Lake, do you want to come out with Mitch, Reed, and Billy for skeet shooting?"

"Oh, Lake, do you want to come out with Kirsty, Gwen, and Kirsty to a musical about Princess Di?"

Back then, Lake wouldn't have looked in my direction if I was *en fuego* and she was holding a perfume extinguisher. But then at a football game she fell from the top of the cheerleader pyramid, jazz hands all the way down.

She Came Plummeting Back to Earth.
She Fell from Grace.
She Leaped from the Nest.
Gravity Is Inevitable.

The ambulance screeched and wailed. It dug ruts across the field. Coach Dhushbak blew his whistle sixty-nine times. There were parents and students crying, parents and students praying, parents and students whispering encouragements, but there was no duct-taping Lake's spine back together. Not even by the cute doctor with the convertible Saab who wrote prescriptions for birth control and acne gel.

I popped another Diet Crank, looked at it, and then poured it into a fern in the hallway.

Almost a year later, when they finally let Lake out of the clinic, she'd undergone a reverse transformation. The rare butterfly-to-caterpillar. She stopped wearing makeup and jewelry. She stopped shaving her legs and her armpits. It freaked all the Kirstys out. The head ones complained, and then lesser Kirstys complained, too. There was a special faculty meeting and Herb had to come to school to remind Principal Whithers about this crazy thing called the Constitution.

For a while, the new Lake was all anyone in school talked about, until they found a girl named Clarissa, rumored pregnant, actually just Häagen-Daz, to dissect instead. But there was a time if Lake McLean did something, no matter how small, everyone else did it, too. Like when she wore a pretzel around her neck on a length of red ribbon and two days later half the girls in school had them hanging in front of their sweaters like tiny beagle turds.

BZZT, BZZZT.

I jumped about twelve feet in the air. If I'd had claws, they would have sunk into the ceiling. I didn't have claws. It was only the bell. I slapped my face a couple of times and then tiptoed downstairs.

"Yo, Sophie!" Herb said, giving me his grin. He wheeled Lake over the threshold and into the living room. "You girls have a rockin' time!"

"You're the best, Herb," I said.

"I'll be back in a couple hours. I got some deliveries."

Herb had started a business in his kitchen, Totally Sweet Rounds, making his own cookies and selling them door-to-door.

"In the middle of the night?"

He gave me the double thumbs. "By day I got kids and moms. After dark, all bets are off with the munchies crowd."

I crouched so Lake could put her arms around my neck, and then carried her up the first flight of stairs. She weighed less than nothing.

"Remember that time you wore that pretzel around your neck?" I whispered. Lake's post-plummet memory could be better, which actually saves her a lot of embarrassment.

"A *pretzel*?"

I held my finger over my lips, taking careful steps by Trish's room. "And then Dayna and all them wore one, too?"

"They *did*?"

I put her on the bed propped with pillows, then went back down to get her chair, taking the stairs three at a time, *bing-bang-bing*.

"Sophie?" Trish called, but I blew by, pretending not to hear.

After the accident, Lake's boyfriend dropped her and her ring-tone friends dropped her, and Dayna Daynes, her best lifelong blood sister, dropped her. Right into my lap. One morning she showed up on the front step. I was too surprised to do anything but stand there all, "Um, can I help you?" and she goes, "You seem interesting, hon. Are you gonna let me in?"

We've been best friends ever since. I keep waiting for her to ask herself why. She says it's weird how you can be a completely different person inside and not realize it. I tell her I can't wait until my Leggy Scandinavian Supermodel bubbles to the surface. She laughs and apologizes about how stuck-up she used to be.

"Oh, Sophie, I'm so sorry, I was such a jerk."

"Yeah, you pretty much were."

"Shut *up*, you're not supposed to agree."

I set her chair back up and she levered herself into it. "So what's the huge emergency?"

I opened my mouth but I could feel myself about to cry.

Lake took my hand and held it. "Just tell me. It's okay, whatever it is."

"The Nurse," I said.

"No way! You're pregnant?"

"No! The Nurse is after me."

Lake burst out laughing. "Oh, my God, hon, you actually had me scared."

My expression didn't change. She stopped laughing. "Yesterday it's a truck, now today it's a nurse?"

I had to admit it sounded astonishingly stupid. "She just sort of . . . appeared."

Lake let go of my hand and rolled back a half inch. "Appeared? Where?"

"In detention. With my dog."

"You don't have a dog."

"I used to."

"What happened to it?"

"It died."

"A magic nurse has your dead dog," she said. It wasn't a question.

"She says I have something of hers, but I don't know what it is."

Lake nodded. Outside there were squealing tires and a faint jingling. I didn't tell her about my father. I already sounded like a lunatic. The rest of the story had to be handed around in little bites, like salmon appetizers.

"I know I sound paranoid."

She didn't bother to deny it.

"I'm scared," I said.

"Of what?"

"Pretty much everything. So can you *please* sleep here tonight?"

If she stayed over I'd have time to explain about my father, maybe let her read Mr. Puglisi's essays. I could tell her about Twinkle. Most of all, I could ask her to come to the lab with me tomorrow. I *had* to go. But there was absolutely no way I could go alone.

Lake sighed. "Sophie, Sophie, perennially at odds with the world."

I sighed back. "Lake, Lake, helping each of us know ourselves better through the miracle of platitude."

She laughed.

Please please please say yes.

Lake lit an unfiltered Winston and blew the smoke through her nose. "How did I end up hanging out with you again?"

"I dunno. Court order?"

She flicked ash in the plant. I waved away the smoke.

"What?" she said.

"Nothing," I said. "Except now all my clothes smell like some guy named Vinnie."

Lake held up a pair of thigh-high latex boots. "You're worried about these?"

I grabbed them from her. "When the big bomb falls and the zombies are roaming in hungry packs and you and I are hiding out in our well-stocked wheelchair-accessible mountain cave, those boots will be our most important possession."

She laughed and put the cigarette out, crushing it between the pages of *Spengler's Beefing Up Your Vocab: 1001 New Words.*

"So are you going to stay, or not?"

"Why don't you go get us some hot chocolate," Lake said, "while I call Daddy."

CHAPTER ELEVEN
OLD SPICE BLUE

A SNEAKY LITTLE SPICE. BIG SPICE

I could only hear every third word. Mostly because I was crouched in the dark, listening through the crack in Sophie's door, hoping for an excuse to be invited in. *Um, there's a fire? Um, do you guys want to order pizza? Um, I just noticed the house's radon levels are dangerously unsafe, maybe we should all go down to my room? Here, Lake, maybe you should hide under these radon-protective blankets. Me? Oh, yeah, sure, I'll get under them, too.*

Meanwhile, Sophie kept saying something about a nurse. Something about Lake sleeping over. Yes, please. Then something about Lake calling her father. I flipped a black cape over my shoulder, twisted my pointy mustache, and tiptoed into the basement. I lifted the extension, slowly released the button, easing in mid-ring like the weaselliest weasel.

"Hello?"

"Daddy?"

"Yeah?

"I'm going to stay at Sophie's tonight."

"Oh, yeah?"

"She's having some problems."

"Problems?"

"Losing it a bit. I get the feeling she wants to go to the lab."

"She does, huh? Anything I can do?"

"No, she just needs someone here with her tonight."

"Hey, you think a cookie would help?"

(Laughing.) "It'll make her paranoid in reverse. She'll start to suspect people are plotting to make her happy."

(Laughing back.) "We may have to try a new direction."

"I know. She keeps talking about how much time she spends on the roof."

"That can be dangerous," Herb said.

There was a click, and then the line went dead.

I crept back up the stairs on my belly. My mother was awake and had actually ventured from her room. I slipped behind the couch, peering over the top, imagining myself on safari at the height of lean season. Oh, man, was it hot on the Serengeti. But I was Shotgun Hemingway and Trish was a rare marsupial foraging for fresh socks and Kleenex. The opportunity to study her was too good to pass up. Through the scope of my Enfield .40 caliber rifle (a Cap'n Gaar's Original Replica Pirate Spyglass) I could see her in what animal behaviorists refer to as the Breakfast Nook. One hand held a saucepan while the other appeared to have trapped and killed a can of tomato soup. She deftly removed red innards from the metallic shell. I could also make out the distinctive crunch of free-range saltine.

Trish stared at her nails for a while and then seemed to fall asleep. Her pan dropped, scraping across the linoleum. She wiped the spill with her slipper, making an It's All Just Chinese to Me face. In the dark, she looked especially pale, preserved, almost beautiful. She'd only dated once since Dad, an Adam's apple-y guy with expensive sunglasses who talked about wedges and roughs and lies. He talked about bringing me over to the course for a few lessons. Trish made an elaborate dinner and then stared into her glass for most of the night. Sunglasses didn't seem worried Mom was about to go facedown in the asparagus. He demonstrated the proper way to hold a fairway wood using a soup ladle. Sophie leaned over and told him she was wearing a leather thong. He shanked one into the rough. She told him I would rather eat a club deep-fried than hit a ball with it. He sliced one into the pond. Then she told him she was wearing a home-arrest ankle bracelet for selling airplane glue to grade-schoolers. Sunglasses never came back.

"You're burning soup," Sophie said, walking into the kitchen and rinsing two mugs. She poured about nine packets of cocoa powder in each. "How do you burn soup?"

Trish pushed back her pillow hair, a blot of soup on her forehead. "I got a disturbing call today."

Sophie looked over and I had to duck.

"From a secretary in the principal's office," Trish said. "She was not asking me to donate to the library fund."

"I swear, it's like I have this big neon arrow on my back," Sophie said. "It's always blinking, *'Find fault with me. Write me a detention slip.'*"

Trish took a spoonful of soup, looked at it distastefully, and put it back in the bowl. "So you're claiming the punishment is undeserved?"

"There are wardrobe concerns," Sophie said. "Coach Dhushbak is a stickler."

"Dhushbak?"

"Dhushbak."

Trish pulled her robe tighter. I could see her imagining a dirty locker room, cold and prescriptionless, and having to change into shorts for laps around the soccer field.

"Besides, um, *Mom?* That call wasn't today. It was a couple of days ago."

Trish blinked. About eighty-four times. Or maybe it was just one really long one.

"Today you were supposed to come in. For a disciplinary conference."

"I was?"

"With Mr. Puglisi."

"Who?"

Who?

"Also? It's my birthday tomorrow."

"Yes, I know," Trish said, clearly not knowing.

"Guess what I want for a present?"

"Things are a little tight at the moment, Sophie. The insurance check is, huge surprise, late again."

"That's fine," Sophie said, "It doesn't cost anything. At least not moneywise."

Trish switched to her It's All Just Albanian to Me face. Sophie got up and pulled the yellow pages off the shelf and started leafing through them, stopping to separate *D* from *E* (I could just make out Dental Hygienist to Endocrine Glands, joined by spattered oatmeal) and *H* from *I* (Halitosis Relief to Indochinese Furniture, joined by a single globule of Smucker's). She stopped at *L* and jabbed her finger onto the page, a small square ad that I could just make out with the spyglass. It was the listing for Fade Labs.

"Anyway, what I want, *Mom*. Actually, what I need, is to go here."

Trish pulled a calcified Kleenex from her robe, unfolded it, and blew her nose. "Mmm-hmmm."

"I know we've had this talk before. Or tried to, and I know I promised not to bring it up again."

"Then don't."

"*Mom*, can you listen, please, for one second? I'm having dreams. About Dad." She help up the phone book, pointing. "I need to go. Like, by tomorrow, after school, latest. So I need you to take me."

"I've already told you —"

Sophie slammed her fist down. A saltshaker fell to the floor. Trish looked up, shocked. I looked up, shocked.

"Mom, have you taken stock of our situation lately? I am losing it. O.S. is the size of an aircraft carrier. You've slept through a presidential election and half a war. It's, like, as a family, I don't think we can keep pretending it's not a little weird Dad disappeared exactly a year ago *on my birthday!*"

Trish got up and poured her soup into the sink. "I'm too tired for this."

"Yeah, it's exhausting," Sophie said. "Flipping channels."

Trish turned, angry. Her eyes were suddenly clear. The fog was gone. Her robe was smooth, her hair miraculously less dented. It was times like this, as she emerged from the depths of Trishdom, that I recognized the mom I grew up with.

"I have no magic answers. Your father didn't leave anything behind but dirty underwear and unpaid bills. People make decisions, and usually they're not thinking about how those decisions affect the rest of us. That's the way the world works. Or the way it doesn't work. So, here we are, you and I, left to wonder. That's it."

"Fine," Sophie said. "But I still need a ride to the lab. Will you be there after school or not?"

"Fine," Trish said. "Happy birthday."

Sophie grabbed her cocoa mugs, spilling some on the floor, and marched back up the stairs. Trish turned, wiped the spill with her slipper, which was too soggy to absorb it, and drifted toward her room.

CHAPTER TWELVE
SOPHIE AND LAKE

THE HIGHER YOU GO, THE HIGHER YOU ARE

O kay, I'll stay," Lake said as I slid back into my room. "On one condition."

I put the mugs down. "What?"

"You take me out on the roof with you."

Spilled cocoa dribbled down my leg. "No way."

Lake started to gather her things. "Okay. If you'd be so kind as to dial for me, I'll let Daddy know he should start warming up the van."

"You don't understand," I said quietly. "It's a tiny space. And I can barely pull myself up."

"Then you better figure out a new method," she said, winding hair around one finger.

"But if you fall —"

"It won't be the first time."

She was testing me. Fine. We were always doing what Lake wanted anyway, the mall, the park, the pool. For once, there was something that I knew about, that was just mine. And it was weird and dangerous. And she needed my help to do it.

"Ding-dong," I said, and pushed open the window. A cool night breeze blew in from three stories down. "Elevator's here."

By putting Lake out first and holding the trim, I was able to squeeze behind her. I stood with one foot on the edge of the sill. There was no room for my other foot. She didn't look so confident as she watched me getting ready to swing up and grip the eaves. It was a one-shot. If I missed, there would be no reaching back.

"Wait!" Lake said, but I'd already let go. I could see black sky between my fingers as they cobbled against the shingles, digging frantically for a grip. My left hand slid, tearing off some skin, but the other held. I pulled myself up the rest of the way.

"Sophie?"

I let out a little yell of surprise, scraping my boots back and forth. A couple of shingles came loose and crashed onto the rocks below.

"SOPHIE!"

I peered back over the edge, laughing.

"You . . . asshole!" she said.

"You still want to come up here?"

She looked down. You could just make out the dumb little statues Trish had put along the walk, a rabbit, a clown, and a lantern-holding jockey.

"You might clear the jockey," I encouraged. "But you'll never make it to those comfy shrubs."

Lake reached up, her mouth set. I lowered the belts I'd stuffed into my waistband. She looped her arms in. I pulled enough so she could grab the eaves, then adjusted position, dragging until she wedged her butt against the two-by-four.

"Oh, my God," she said.

"What?"

"This is the single greatest thing ever."

Lights twinkled all the way out to the strip malls along the highway. Cars rumbled slowly through town, their high beams vibrating, like pigs sniffing for truffles.

"My father used to bring me up here and point out constellations," I said. "He'd go 'We're in the sky together, sweetie. I'm the string and you're the kite.'"

"That is so . . . disgustingly sappy," Lake said.

"There's way worse I haven't told you." I laughed. "You have no idea."

"Maybe it's not me you should tell."

"What's that supposed to mean?" I asked.

Lake leaned back and crossed her arms. "It's all right to see someone, you know."

"See?"

"Like a doctor. Pills and stuff."

"Unbelievable," I said. "Even you?"

She made an effort to brighten her face. "Listen, it's just that I worry when —"

I stood up and stuck one foot out, letting it dangle over the edge. I spread my arms and tilted my head back.

"See?" she said. "This is exactly the sort of thing I was talking about."

"I bet you a hundred bucks," I said, my stomach all swervy, "if I do a swan dive onto the front steps? I'll wake up tomorrow, and everything will be fine."

Lake grabbed my ankle. Instead of helping, it made me start to lose my balance.

"Hey!" I said, but she kept pulling.

"Stop it!" she said.

"Don't!" I said, falling a degree at a time. She squeezed my ankle, but there was no way she could hold me. And there was nothing for me to grab. I could see over the edge of the roof. I didn't want to fall. But then, you know, I sort of did. I closed my eyes, weightless.

"Oh, man, what in *hell* are you guys doing?"

O.S. grabbed my arm and swung me back onto the shingles until I lay flat.

"You're here!" I said, breathing hard.

"Of course I'm here," he said angrily. "I mean, where else would I be?"

"You sister is nuts," Lake said.

He nodded. "I mean, is my sister nuts?"

"It's okay, though," I laughed. "I have a great medical plan. I even have my own private nurse."

Lake lit a cigarette. The three of us stared out at the cars and stores and cul-de-sacs while her smoke rose up in one long plume.

CHAPTER THIRTEEN
MR. PUGLISI

THE DAY MY FATHER DISAPPEARED, ESSAY #3

The next morning I came early, since Trish was going to pick us up right after school, but Mr. Puglisi wasn't there. I waited twenty minutes. There was a new poster on the wall. It was a picture of an infant in its mother's arms, nestled between her enormous breasts. Underneath it said *I'm So Happy, I Could Shit Myself.*

I took out my essay. And put it in my lap. Another twenty minutes went by. No Mr. Puglisi. I picked it up and harrumphed a few times before reading it out loud.

> It was late at night, and we were still lying in bed. O.S. was snoring. I was half listening to the hum of Trish's TV when I heard a car pull up to the house. It skidded to a stop. I went to the top of the steps. My father ran up from the basement, slamming the door.
>
> My mother watched from the kitchen, holding a casserole dish, about to ask a question. My father took off his lab coat and threw it in the corner, holding up one hand for silence. He loosened his tie. There was a knock, polite and then rude. It got louder. The bell rang. Bzzz bzzz bzzz.

O.S. was still asleep. My father took a deep breath and opened the door.

Officer Goethe, with his big ape-shoulders, was standing there, looking even bigger than usual. Two other men in suits and sunglasses stood behind him.

"Where is it?" Officer Goethe asked.

"Where's what?"

Officer Goethe almost smiled. "Computers say she brought something out. Not code, but something real. Since it ain't in the office, that means you took it with you. And now you're going to give it back."

"I have no idea what you're talking about," my father said, and then the three men pushed their way in, taking my father by the arms.

"What are you doing?" my mother asked.

"We have a few more questions," Officer Goethe said.

"Everyone always has a few more questions," my mother said.

Out the window, I could see the men putting my father in the backseat of a sedan, next to a woman in a white uniform, before it sped away.

I stopped reading, alone in the office, actually wishing Mr. Puglisi had shown up. I put the essay on his desk, which was empty except for cookie crumbs and a manila envelope. On the front of the envelope was written *Sophie Blue, Progress Report.* Underneath was a drawing of a cake full of candles. It wasn't half bad. Beneath that, it said *Happy Birthday!* The office was silent and dark. I couldn't hear anything in the hallway, no kids, no slamming lockers. I counted to six, saying, "Don't do it" each time, and then grabbed the envelope and tore it open. It was one page. Written on it, in red marker, were three words. That was my progress report. Three words.

Beware The Nurse.

CHAPTER FOURTEEN
KENNY FADE

BY ONES TO ELEVEN, WINNERS OUT. WAY OUT

Kenny and Freckle took turns dunking. The rest of the team was at the other end of the court, being yelled at by Coach Dhushbak. Workmen were repairing the wall in the corner where a delivery truck had smashed into it, leaving a pile of dust and cinder blocks and snapped two-by-fours, so Kenny was allowed to just watch. Actually, he was pretty much allowed to shoot baskets or sit on the bench or blow off practice altogether and make out with Dayna under the big oak tree behind the gym whenever he felt like it. Mostly, he didn't feel like it.

"Bet you can't make fifteen left-handed jumpers in a row," Freckle said.

Kenny made fourteen left-handed jumpers in a row. When he missed the fifteenth, Freckle said, "You suck."

The two of them played Horse; Kenny won. They played Kentucky Horse, and Kenny won. They played Around the World, Twenty-one, and One on One. Kenny won. After, when they were sweating under the stanchion, watching Coach yell at some scrub for messing up a pick and roll, Kenny turned to Freckle.

"Can I tell you something serious for a minute?"

Freckle popped a can of Sour White. "Sure."

"There is something really and desperately wrong with me."

Freckle laughed, sweeping hair from his forehead. "Yeah,

there's a ton wrong with you. You're a mess. You got it so tough, I don't know how you manage to get up every day, let alone soldier on."

"No, I mean it," Kenny said, scratching his elbow. On the wall above the bleachers was a poster of a thin woman in a bikini holding two huge, melting ice cream cones. Underneath it said *Eat It Now, or You May Have to Eat It Later.*

Freckle stopped smiling. "Okay, lay it on me."

"For one thing, maybe I'm being paranoid, but people keep going through my stuff."

"Souvenirs. They want a little piece of the Fa-day."

"I feel sick," Kenny said. "I've felt this way for weeks. Like I've eaten too many marshmallows."

"Maybe you should lay off Dayna for a while," Freckle said. "She's enough to put a diabetic in a coma."

"And sometimes I hear voices. Like a girl's voice? In my head."

"Man, I *hope* Dayna's making noises. Otherwise, you're totally doing something wrong."

"Dude, I'm serious," Kenny said.

Freckle sat up straight. "Sorry. No more jokes."

"Dayna and I were fooling around yesterday."

"So?"

"I didn't . . . I didn't want to."

Freckle looked appalled. "But that's like saying you don't want to *breathe.*"

"All I could think about was that I really wanted to pick up her clothes."

"What?" Freckle said. "And like, sniff 'em? Really get your nose in there and smell the action?"

"No," Kenny said. "Like, wear them. Like, get dressed and look at myself in the mirror."

Freckle stared at Kenny for a long time. "No way."

"I know."

"Um —"

Kenny waved. "I don't blame you if you don't want to hang out anymore."

"Dude," Freckle said, putting his hand on Kenny's shoulder. "C'mon."

"Thanks," Kenny said, tightening the laces on his Dikes. "I knew you were the only one who would listen. I just had to tell somebody."

Kenny got up, dribbling the ball to the other end. His teammates cheered, slapping his back. Coach Dhushbak rolled out the game ball. "The big gun is here now, people."

Twee.

The team ran up and down the court, random plops of sweat and the chirp of sneaker against varnish, the screech of elbow against floor. They went like that for half an hour, no one giving an inch, Coach Dhushbak yelling out the score. With thirty seconds left, Kenny knocked down his twelfth consecutive basket, a nifty up-and-under reverse, to put his side ahead. He backpedaled down the floor. Freckle reached out to high-five, when Kenny's face constricted. He stumbled and then collapsed. Everyone laughed, thinking it was a joke, Kenny just loosening things up. Kenny showing everyone that, even in the heat of battle, they were still all on the same team. Even Coach Dhushbak laughed, saying, "All right, Fade, let's get 'er up and finish this thing." After a while, though, when he didn't, no one laughed anymore. Zac touched Kenny's Air Dike with the tip of his sneaker, and when Kenny didn't move, Coach Dhushbak ran into his office to call an ambulance.

CHAPTER FIFTEEN
SOPHIE "GOTHIKA" BLUE

KETCHUP IS A VEGETABLE

I wheeled Lake into line. She grabbed a sticky yellow tray, handed me one, and filled hers with pizza and chocolate milk. I put mine back.

"So now you're on a hunger strike?"

I ignored her. After the roof, she'd refused to talk about anything that had to do with a truck or a nurse. She and O.S. sat on the floor and played cards. Even after they fell asleep, I stayed up all night, thinking about the lab.

"Aren't you tired?"

"Not at all."

I figured there was a good chance Trish wouldn't show after school. We needed Herb to drive us in the van. I needed to think of a way to ask.

"Herb is not driving us in the van," Lake said.

I opened my pad and drew aimlessly.

"Maybe you should collect some of his hair. Make a voodoo doll out of it."

I looked down. I'd been drawing Aaron Agar. I hooked my arm around so she couldn't see.

"There's your brother," Lake pointed. "Why don't you invite him over?"

O.S. was sitting in the freshman section with his friend, the weird little German guy who looked like a rabbit.

"Why don't you?"

"Just do it."

I stood and waved.

O.S. walked over and immediately started talking about comics. Lake pretended to care. Artists and heroes and villains and sidekicks. He reached in his bag and showed her his favorite issue. It was about a woman in a white outfit. Under her picture, in bloodred letters, it said *La Nutrika*. He opened to the centerfold, a drawing of La Nutrika in a tight nurse's uniform.

"Holy total fuck!"

I grabbed the comic out of his hand.

"Hey!" O.S. said. "Give it back!"

On the next page, La Nutrika was directing a team of factory workers with a whip in one hand and a schematics manual in the other. The workers were building a huge metal circle in the middle of a burned-out factory.

"Why's that one your favorite?" Lake asked, trying to cover for my weirdness.

I flipped back a few pages. There was a fat scientist sweating all over the place, barking orders. Then robot stuff. A robot flying through the roof of the building. Some nerdy boy in a trench coat who was sort of cute. I turned to the last page. The lab was new, gleaming. It was like a sweatshop. The big circle was finished. Inside the circle was a membrane, like soap glistening in the middle of a bubble wand. People were loading microwaves and sneakers and televisions into trucks as they came through the membrane. *This* was what The Nurse wanted?

"Because my father gave it to me," O.S. answered.

No way. Uh-uh.

I felt frozen shards of ice along my sides. I slid my chair against his, grabbing his arm and squeezing hard.

"Jeez, calm down."

"When did Dad —?"

Donk.

Zac Grace elbowed O.S. in the back of the head. He was followed by Aaron Agar and half the basketball team.

"Hey!" O.S. said, looking up. When he saw it was Zac, he looked back down.

"Hey, dog," Zac grinned, his dumb hair gelled forward. He wore a yellow silk tracksuit. "I hear you're trying out for the team this year! All signed up and ready to do some balling?"

O.S. didn't answer, pinching his milk carton. A bubble rose in the straw, suspended midway, trapped. I looked at Aaron, who avoided my eye.

"What's O.S. stand for, anyhow?" Zac asked loudly. "Orgasm Supplier? Obese City?"

"Actually fairly clever," O.S. said. "I mean, the second one?"

"Hey, Oral Slurp," someone called. "What's it like having Columbine-a for a sister?"

"Must suck!" someone else answered.

"Yo, dude, watch it, she's got an Uzi!"

Some kids ducked under their tables. Others held their chests and keeled over like they'd been shot.

"Could you possibly be any more of a renob?" I said.

Zac put his hands on O.S.'s shoulders and squeezed. "What does that even mean?"

"I believe it's boner backward," O.S. said with a wince. "But I could be wrong."

"That's sheer genius," Zac said. "Hey, do you know what this spells?" He stood back, pretending he was holding pom-poms, and then acted out letters like he was leading a cheer, *Gimme a T, gimme an E, T-E-S-T T-U-B-E.*

The cafeteria exploded with laughter. Zac took a deep bow. I stood, not knowing if I was going to run or hit Zac over the head with a tray. Aaron looked at me. He sort of shrugged, not even flinching as the Popsicle truck slammed through the plateglass window behind him, roaring like a cornered animal. No one ran. No one screamed.

"Dad? Is it really you?"

"Yeah, it's really me," Zac laughed. "I'm so your daddy."

The truck crushed chairs and books and the faculty table, coming right at O.S. I stood in front of him, spreading my arms, waiting for the grill to connect with the center of my chest.

CHAPTER SIXTEEN
KENNY FADE

ANEURISM, INFARCTION, CLOT, SHUNT, SUTURE, IMPINGEMENT, BIOPSY

Kenny awoke on a cot in a white hospital room. A TV mounted to the wall played *Spin My Fortune.* Buzzers buzzed and lights flashed and someone won a couch shaped like a donkey, and then someone else traded a year's supply of cinnamon Toast-R Shangles for six tubes of Leggy Leg Waxy Wax.

A candy striper came in to fluff Kenny's pillow. She had black hair down to her waist, a tight white skirt, and white pumps. She looked like she'd been ordered out of a beer ad.

"How you doin', sweetie?" she asked.

Kenny probed his stomach with one finger, which brought up the taste of rotten marshmallow so strong he gagged. "Not so hot."

The candy striper tsk'd, leaning over to tuck his sheet on the other side, brushing her enormous juggs against his chest and arm. She straightened up and stroked Kenny's cheek. "Maybe you need a sponge bath, huh?"

Before Kenny could answer, Dayna came in, followed by Rose. Dayna and the candy striper sized each other up. The candy striper straightened her tiny outfit, so tiny there were no wrinkles to straighten, and reluctantly left.

"How are you, honey?" Rose asked, lighting a cigar. She laid a platter of cookies on the table next to Kenny's IV hanger.

"You probably can't smoke in here," Kenny said. On the wall

behind her was a poster of a crumbling coal factory. Underneath it said *I Used to Smoke, Too.*

"Zac and Freckle are in the waiting room," Dayna cooed, rubbing Kenny's neck and chest. "They're *so* worried." Her hand went down under the sheet, groping around, like she was looking for something.

Rose winked. "Need me to leave for a bit?"

Kenny grabbed Dayna's hand as the doctor walked in. He had a huge head and big round teeth. He held a chart and looked it over, flipping pages, making harrumphing sounds.

"Well, doc?" Kenny asked, already knowing it was cancer. That would finally, blessedly, explain everything. He was almost hoping for it. The movie of the rest of his life played in his head, sad music, a crying Dayna, his mother knitting a tan wig for when he lost his hair to chemo, and then a trip to Disney World before he succumbed to an orchestral soundtrack.

"Not a darn thing." The doctor smiled. "You're in perfect health."

Dayna cheered. Down the hall, they could hear the candy striper cheer. Kenny's stomach rolled. "That's not possible. There's definitely something wrong with me."

"Nope," the doctor said, a trickle down his forehead. "Nothing."

"I think you should do a few more tests."

"Hey, maybe you should listen to the doctor," Rose said. "Doctor knows best."

"No. Wait."

"Why don't we close the door?" Rose said. Her white dress glowed.

"You're lying, aren't you?" Kenny demanded.

"Sorry," the doctor said, backing away.

Rose grabbed Kenny by the arm, raising her lip. "Where is it?"

"Where's what?"

Dayna moved toward the bed. When Kenny tried to sit, Rose held him down. They pulled up his gown and Kenny began to scream, his voice sounding just like a little girl's.

CHAPTER SEVENTEEN
THE NURSE

ESSENTIAL MEMO: CLASSIFIED

FROM: The Nurse

TO: Code Production, IT Unit, Chip Design Team, Theoretics Research Team, Town Council, Lab Workers, Factory Workers, and On-site Techs

RE: Voluntary Production Unit Force, the Virtuality v. 2

As you all may know, we have finally finished Beta cycle and full testing procedure for Bio-Rite IV, and the time has come to enact full usage of Voluntary Production Unit Force, or VPUF, within the Virtuality, and put the entire grid online for inspection by the investment team arriving from Beijing in forty-eight hours. Tangible product MUST begin rolling into the warehouse immediately. Ignition has taken place. The Original Sample is in hand, and this office expects all teams to have production cycles complete within twenty-four hours. When the Proof has been secured, production will commence immediately. Triple shifts are expected. Failure to comply will result in immediate placement on Voluntary Production Unit Force.

Hey, don't fuck with me.

The Nurse

CHAPTER EIGHTEEN
KENNY FADE

ARE WE THERE YET, ARE WE THERE YET,
DADDY, ARE WE THERE YET?

enny Fade opened his eyes, still screaming, except instead of lying in a hospital bed he was standing in the doorway of a vacuum repair store. A sign on the wall said Brick's Fix Your Hoover in dingy red letters. Upright vacuums stood in a group, like schoolkids waiting for the bus. Chrome attachments and coils of hose hung from the ceiling in rows. In the corner, a broken-down soda machine hummed loudly. It was the old kind with knobs and neon pipettes, and a nickel coin slot. Across the front it said *Sour White*.

"Hello?"

Under a dingy lamp was an old Formica desk, covered with parts and rusty tools. At the desk stood a man with an enormous head and a crappy old sweater. Behind him was a poster of a society woman standing in a coffin. She was holding a poodle in one hand and a diamond in the other. *You Can't Take It With You* was written underneath.

"Hi," the guy said. "Welcome to the Virtuality. I'm Brick, your counterman and Central Scrutinizer."

Kenny took a step forward and rubbed his eyes. It was the doctor. "Sorry, I'm a little dazed. Are we still in the hospital?"

"Actually, Piece, you were never at the hospital."

Kenny cleared his throat. "Where's Dayna? And Rose?"

Brick thought about it. "That's a tricky philosophical question,

Piece. *Where* are they? Where *were* they? Were *they* even they? We could spend all afternoon on it."

Kenny put his elbows on the counter. "Why do you keep calling me Piece?"

Brick conked himself with a roller brush. "Sorry. I'm working on my street lingo. It's a subroutine called Generation Bridge. I came up with *Piece* myself. As in piece of the puzzle. Like how we all are one, whether we want to be or not."

"You're not really a doctor, are you?" Kenny asked.

Brick nodded. "Yeah, sorry, Chief. That's just a role I have to play. The doctor here, the therapist there. Tons of lines to remember. Plus, the program's really buggy. Half the time I'm just fixing code."

"You're making zero sense," Kenny said, holding both arms over his head and forming a big zero.

Brick pinched his eyelid. "Okay, why don't we start at the beginning?"

"Good idea."

"For one thing, you are so totally dead."

Kenny looked down at his feet, his big red size-thirteen Dikes. They didn't feel dead.

"Freckle and Zac, right? They gave you twenty bucks to pull my chain?"

"Nope," Brick said. "This is the Returns Department. It's where you go when being dead doesn't take."

"Hey, ASSHATS!" Kenny yelled. "You can come out now."

When no one came out, Kenny started to get scared. The man with the enormous head stared at him.

"But I've never been here in my life."

Brick finished the assembly of an intake valve and laid it carefully next to a pile of tiny motors.

"It's true, you've never been here in your life. But you have been here in someone else's. A bunch of times."

CHAPTER NINETEEN
KENNY'S DEAD

ROCK, PAPER, SCISSORS, DEAD,
ROCK, PAPER, SCISSORS, ROCK

S o this is supposed to be heaven?" Kenny said.

Brick tapped his nose with a screwdriver. "Well, that's one way to look at it. Depending, you know, on your preferred text. There's Old Testament thunder and plagues. There's the New Testament routine, which, to be honest, goes a bit overboard with the leper-kissing. We've also got a Koran *Oasis and Figs* simulation I could boot up. And, of course, there's the Nietzsche *Dark And Lonely Room* package, although people keep complaining there aren't enough candles. It's all in the catalog."

"What catalog?"

"The one you read before you spin the big wheel."

Brick pulled aside a curtain. Behind him was a huge game show wheel with names of occupations written inside different colored triangles, like FRENCH REVOLUTION GUILLOTINE OPERATOR and UNDERGROUND GRAPHIC ARTIST and MOM OF SIX DIFFICULT CHILDREN and TANNED CELEBRITY GYNECOLOGIST and HOT SHIT YOUNGER BROTHER and CROUCHING BEHIND A WALL AT WACO and SPEEDO SEWING TECHNICIAN and MENOPAUSAL SEATTLE POETESS and LEADER OF ZOMBIE RESISTANCE. The last one just said U PICK 'EM.

"I'm in the mental ward, aren't I?"

Brick raised his eyebrows. "Most people can't wait to take a spin at being someone else. No more paying bills, no more trudging to the bus in the snow. Teachers? Parents? Bullies? Gone." He spun the wheel as a demonstration. A red stopper clicketyclacked on the pegs, finally landing on FIRST PLUMBER TO SCALE EVEREST.

"So?"

"So you take a spin, drink a can of code, and shut your eyes. We play the best movie ever made, where you're the lead character, over and over again. Most people lie back and enjoy it. But you, Chief? For some reason, you keep turning the projector off."

Kenny pressed his temples with the palms of his hands. "So was I just Keith Richards? John Holmes? The King of Siam?"

Brick laughed. "This time? You were you. Being Kenny *was* your fantasy. The whole basketball thing? The whole Dayna and her tight outfit deal?" Brick winked and gave Kenny a thumbsup. "Nice spin. Hot piece of code."

Kenny decided he was definitely still in the hospital. They'd given him the wrong drugs. It was time to find a doctor who wasn't insane and could fill him with the right drugs.

"Don't," Brick said.

Kenny walked to the front door. He grabbed the handle, flung it open, and almost stepped into blackness. Except within that blackness brilliant constellations winked, so close he could almost reach out and poke them. There were pink nebulae, meteors, huge swirling galaxies puffing with dust. His foot dangled out over a welcome mat that floated in the doorway. It was missing letters so that it just spelled *elco.*

"I'm in a vacuum store," Kenny said, almost laughing. "In the middle of *space*?"

"I know, I know," Brick said.

"Okay," Kenny admitted, trying to calm himself. "The whole basketball team thing? And Dayna? And being popular and all? It did feel sort of . . . fake. I mean, it was fun, but there was definitely something off."

"Now you're talking."

Kenny nodded. "You know, it sounds weird, but I actually feel a little better. I mean, at least things are finally making *some* kind of sense. I pretty much thought I was losing it."

"Keep that new understanding in mind, dude, 'cause there's this one other thing? The thing I haven't mentioned yet? You might want to sit down."

"What," Kenny said, not sitting, "could possibly be more ridiculous than what you've already told me?"

"Ready?"

"Ready."

"You, dude, are a girl."

Kenny gave Brick the finger.

"Hey, now," Brick said.

Kenny walked over to a display of chrome suction tubes and looked at his reflection, for once clean and clear as day. He seemed to be about eighteen. And a whole lot shorter. With dyed black hair and dumb Goth-bangs and a Doktah Jack and the Kevorkians tour shirt that held a pair of perky breasts. It was true. It was totally, completely true.

He was a freaking girl.

CHAPTER TWENTY
SOPHIE IN THE LIGHT

THE STORY WITHIN THE STORY WITHIN THE STORE

Actually, dude, your name is Sophie. Though some people call you Gothika. Or Columbine-a. Or Test . . ."

"Yeah, I get it," Sophie said.

"Kenny Fade? Doesn't exist. Well, there *is* a Kenny, but that'd be your younger brother. You spun a fantasy version of his life, where he's good-looking and athletic and so forth."

Old Spice? She was just Old Spice?

"But my Kenny has no friends. My Kenny weighs three hundred pounds. My Kenny reads comic books."

"True," Brick said. "Reads them and collects them and hides them under his bed."

Sophie thought about it. "If everything that just happened was a fantasy, who was Dayna?"

"Dayna was code, Babe." Brick laughed. "She was a code babe. A numeric variable based on your memories. You know an actual Dayna, yes? And the others that made their way into your fantasy? A freckled boy, for instance?"

Sophie blushed.

"Memories gather around the Personality Formulate like ivy."

"But I was just in the caf two seconds ago," Sophie said. "How could I have been Kenny Fade all that time? All the games and classes and driving around in a Jeep?"

Brick smiled proudly. "Your Kenny-ness was about a minute and a half of program, running-time wise. While you're standing there blinking, or sort of staring into space, a whole life can unfold. The clock moves exponentially faster in the Virtuality."

Sophie began touching herself randomly, which seemed vaguely illegal, still getting used to having contours. She ran her hands along her sides, over her bra and down her back. Kenny Fade's memories fell like something melting onto her neck, the team, school, Dayna, Zac.

"It almost *was* like I could feel myself banging around in that big, lanky boy," she whispered.

"Yeah, that shouldn't happen," Brick said sheepishly. "We're working on it. Code overflow. Platform issues."

Little amounts of Sophie began seeping back in as well. Trish, Lake, school. Her classes. The Rumor. She looked at Brick again. Her jaw started to pulse. He had an enormous head and there was a big hole in his sweater.

"Wait a minute — Mr. *Puglisi*?"

Brick blushed, from the chin up. He slowly turned the nameplate on his desk around. It said Brick Puglisi in big block letters.

"Your first name is Brick?"

"It wasn't my choice," he admitted.

"But what are you doing here?"

"I work here. I'm *The Counselor 2.0*."

"But what about your office? What about school?"

"Never been. You came to see me." He pointed at a door in the corner that said *Counselor's Office*.

Sophie thought about it. She'd never actually seen Mr. Puglisi in the hallway, had never seen him at lunch or the faculty table or talking to other students. A rush of stark cold madness surged through her, from her toes all the way to her hairline.

He giggled. "How's it feel? You're dead *and* you're nuts."

It was true, Sophie thought. She was crazy as a shit-throwing monkey. "So why tell me all this now?"

"It's your birthday," Mr. Puglisi said. "Time for you to go back and fulfill your purpose."

"What if I don't want to go back?"

Mr. Puglisi looked over his shoulder, and then leaned in.

"Dead? Not dead? Software? Reality? That's for your Kants and Humes and Spinozas. Your hippies and self-helpers and evangelists. Bottom line, your injection has spent a year gestating, and now you're ready. We all, in the end, have a purpose."

"What's mine?"

"From what I understand, you've already been told."

Sophie closed her eyes. The Nurse. Go to the lab. Picture book. Nutrika.

"Bringing her Kenny's comic book? *That's* my great purpose?"

Mr. Puglisi shrugged. He put his finger on the big wheel. "Ready to spin?"

"No."

"Do it anyway."

Sophie leaned over and flicked it with her middle finger. The wheel tore around clockwise, the red flipper clacking maniacally. EMBEZZLING ACCOUNT MANAGER went by. For an agonizing second the flipper rested on TUNA BARGE GUTTER AND SCALER before falling one last notch to NO CHANGE.

"Wow," Mr. Puglisi said. "What are the odds?"

"So I'll be me?" Sophie asked. "Not anyone special?"

"But you *are* special."

"Go screw."

Mr. Puglisi reached into his pocket for a nickel. He yanked a can of Sour White from the ancient soda machine. "Liquid code. Doesn't work without it."

The rim was crusty and smelled like ammonia. Sophie held it to her lips, the soda hot and cold at the same time. It tasted like bad milk and burning plastic and antifreeze and raw sugar. It also made her very, very nauseous, which was just like old times. Old Kenny Fade times. She closed her eyes and felt herself slipping . . . in.

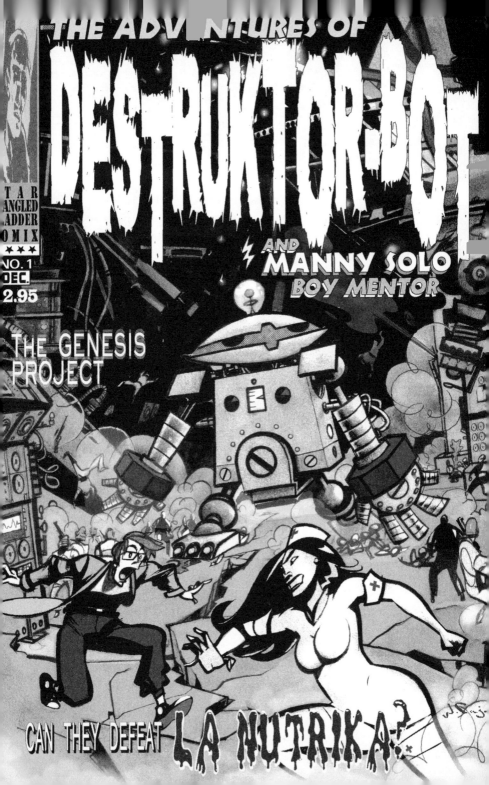

CHAPTER TWENTY
LAKE MCLEAN

KETCHUP IS A VEGETABLE

Sophie wheeled me into the caf grumpy and medieval-looking, still pouting from the night before.

People at the tables around us were having fun, laughing, joking. It was a rowdy Friday, sunny outside. Sophie didn't join in, or even look up, hunched over her sketch pad, going seriously *GQ* on Aaron Agar.

"Maybe you should collect some of his hair," I said. "Make a voodoo doll."

She ignored me. Or maybe she was trying to decide whether or not to give me the finger.

Her brother sat at a table across from us with the guy who pretended to be German. "Why don't you invite him over?" I said.

"Who, Aaron?" she said, alarmed.

"No, Kenny."

Sophie gave a halfhearted wave.

Kenny walked over and put down a stack of funny books that spread out like a deck of cards. One slid in front of me.

"This any good?"

"A classic," he beamed, spinning it so I could see better. "The early *Ion Crusher Wolf* rules."

"Tell me about it."

He looked up for a second, not sure how enthusiastic to be. "You mean *tell me about it*, like, please explain more, or *tell me about it,* like, you already know what I'm talking about so please stop boring you?'

I smiled. "Please explain more."

"Um, well, the Razor Rodriguez stuff on *Amazin' Kid Kabul?* Oh, man, that's some awesome art. And then there's this new series, *Suck* . . . well, never mind about that. Anyway, I prefer more obscure titles, like *Tasty Carpet Tales,* or *Connoisseur Mannoisseur.*"

I readjusted my chair while he pulled a comic from heavy plastic. "This, though, is my favorite."

The cover showed a thick-jawed robot shooting laser beams from its eyes while standing atop a pile of unconscious henchmen. Kenny opened to the centerfold, which was a nurse in a fighting crouch, her hands up like a cat's claws. It was actually beautifully drawn. Sophie's head snapped up, her mouth wide open.

Kenny held out one finger. "See, Manny Solo, who I suppose you would call Destruktor-Bot's sidekick, although I've always found that to be a derogatory —"

Sophie snatched the comic from her brother, practically tearing it in half.

"Why is that one your favorite?" I asked as he thumbed his glasses back in place.

"There's only one of them. None of the comic shops have even heard of it. Is it extremely valuable? Definitely."

"Like, on eBay?"

"Yeah, but I would . . . but I would never sell it."

"Why not?

He took an enormous bite of sandwich. "Because my father gave it to me?"

Sophie almost threw a gear. "Wait a minute. This is important. When did Dad . . . ?"

Donk.

It was classic Zac, showing off for the Kirstys, trying to embarrass me without doing it directly. He gave me a wink and then did a little cheerleader routine. The entire caf erupted in laughter. Sophie stood, about to say something. And then froze. She was staring over Zac's shoulder. Everyone waited. Sophie began to blink, slowly at first and then really fast. She finally turned and lurched out of the cafeteria.

"Later for you," Zac said, twirling his finger around his ear. I put my palms against Kenny's thigh, which turned him maroon, and pushed as hard as I could. My chair slammed into Zac's knee. A few trays went flying, beans and cheese, a tortilla, some hot sauce. Zac yowled, jumping up and down.

"Oh, I'm sorry."

"You *bitch*," he growled. I smiled sweetly. Miss Last got up from her pimiento loaf and chips and walked over from the faculty table. Zac swore under his breath and limped toward the opposite door.

"Say hi to Tinky for me," I called.

"It's the anniversary today?" Kenny explained as people went back to their business. "Of my dad and everything?"

I stared at him for a minute. "Is there a reason you phrase every single thing you ever say as question?"

He thumbed his glasses. "Poor nutrition?"

I laughed. "I didn't realize you and Zac were such pals."

Kenny swirled his milk philosophically. "He spit on me once? Last year. On my favorite shirt. I mean, who spits on someone? What part of the brain does that impulse even come from?"

"I don't know, hon. Maybe he had a hard upbringing."

"That seems unlikely," Kenny said, chewing. "I believe his parents live in a rather large house and, you know, given the cost of new pairs of Air Dikes and so forth . . ."

"I was being facetious."

Kenny's eyes widened. "Oh, I . . ."

The bell rang. He formed a *V* with the pizza crust and snow-plowed the entire thing into his mouth, then slid his Death-Bot magazine back into its plastic sleeve.

"Um, about this field trip to the lab? Are we really going?"

"We?"

His entire head flushed red. "Um . . ."

"Yes," I said. "It's a date."

CHAPTER NINETEEN
SOPHIE BLUE

DON'T FORGET TO CLAMP THE UMBILICAL

The soda coats my throat like oil, like burning ammonia. I close my eyes and there's a wetness, a slickness, a sickly warmth. I am naked, in a tube, compressed, tightened, like being inside a long, thin Ziploc, stretched and filled with warm syrup. But it hurts, too, being pulled, being pushed, being dragged. I cannot breathe, and yet I can, big gulps of liquid that is somehow air, somehow numbers, all of it flashing by. I cannot open my eyes, but I can see, my lids not thick enough to block out the red glow, the pink glow, the wet glow, and then I am hurtling along in the tube, ten miles an hour, fifty, a hundred, a thousand, slick, weightless, dizzy-sick.

And then I howl.

It's like sliding between metaphorical legs.

Like being born again.

0001010100101010.

I opened my eyes in the hallway outside the caf, shaking. Through the heavy glass doors, I could see Zac Grace standing in front of our table, the one with O.S. and Lake, except I wasn't with them. I was and then I wasn't. It was like blinking and then being a mile away. Bang. I could see Zac waving his arms and laughing, then Lake did something with her chair, moving backward. Zac swore, holding his knee while Miss Last walked over. O.S. laughed. Lake batted her eyes. Neither seemed to notice I was gone. I leaned against a row of lockers, sick to my stomach and sweating. I wasn't dead. I wasn't anywhere, except where I'd always been.

Right here, from head-to-ass crazy.

I couldn't go back in. I couldn't go to class. I couldn't go see . . .

Wait a minute.

I turned and walked down the hallway, at first slowly, so as not to jinx anything. But my legs couldn't help themselves, moving faster, my feet moving faster.

Please be there, please be there, please be there.

My boots clomped on the tiles. They echoed in the doorways.

Please be there, please be there, please be there.

I took a left by Biology, down the long corridor, *clomp. Squeak.* And then a quick right. *Clomp. Squeak.*

I was full-out running, one more left, sliding sideways at least ten feet before banging into a locker, hard. I was in the middle of the hallway.

It put me directly in front of Mr. Puglisi's office.

And there was nothing there but a cinder-block wall.

Not even a door.

CHAPTER EIGHTEEN
AARON "FRECKLE" AGAR

FREKLEO MONTAGUE AND SOPHELET CAPULET

He followed her between the tables, through the pointing and laughter, then through the big metal doors into the hallway. He stood for a moment at a safe distance, while she bent over as if she were going to collapse, wondering what to do. Say something? Not say something? Give her space? Rush over to help? She suddenly turned and began to walk. He kept up while she jogged and then practically sprinted in her big, clompy boots. He followed until she stood in front of the wall across from the bio lab, staring at a row of whitewashed cinder blocks.

"Hey, are you okay?"

She didn't answer, so he gently put his hand on her shoulder. She whirled around like a cat ready to sink fang. Her face was sweaty and confused. He stepped back.

"I just, um . . . I thought . . ."

"I'm sorry," she said, wiping her eyes, which smeared mascara sideways. It was actually sort of hot.

"It's okay," Aaron said. "What were you looking at?"

Sophie turned away from the wall, embarrassed. "I thought there was a door here."

Aaron rapped his knuckles against the cinder block. "Feels pretty solid."

"Don't bother pretending," Sophie said. "I know it doesn't make any sense."

Maybe she really was as loony as everyone said, he thought. But so what? He couldn't stop staring at her face, now that he was finally this close. He'd been working on finding excuses to be near her for a year, but she never gave any sign she wanted him to, always hunched over her drawings or kicking something with her boots. He considered putting his arm around her, since she was still shivering, but offered his jacket instead. Sophie took it and slid it over her shoulders.

"Listen, I just wanted to come and say . . . you know. I thought that whole thing in there wasn't . . . I guess, cool. I mean, I didn't think. And then when? I guess mostly . . ."

He knew he sounded like a fool. Mumbling on and on. *Get down to basics, guy!* he told himself. Grow a sac and just say it!

"Okay, for one thing, Zac is a total asshole."

She smirked. "But you're on the team together."

"I know. I think I'm gonna quit."

"Really?"

Aaron shrugged. "Yeah, really."

Sophie straightened her skirt. "You sure you want to be seen standing here?"

"In the hall?"

"With me. Next to me."

"I don't care," Aaron said. "What people are. You know. Thinking."

"Oh, you don't?"

"No. Do you?"

Sophie stared for a minute, waiting for the whole thing to be a setup. Waiting for Aaron to burst out laughing or make a joke, say something ironic and then call his friends over.

"You left this in there," he finally said, holding a piece of paper rolled into a cone. Sophie took it and let it fall open. It was the picture she'd drawn of him.

"Oh. My. God."

She crumpled it up and threw it onto the floor.

"But I *like* it," he said, smoothing the paper over his thigh. "You're freaking talented."

The bell rang, clanging in the empty hallway, incredibly loud. Kids began to scramble out of the cafeteria, out of classrooms. In a minute, they'd come rushing around the corner. The hallway would be teeming. Sophie didn't want to go to class. She didn't want to go anywhere that wasn't exactly where Aaron was going. She hoped he was thinking the same thing.

"Hey," came a voice from behind them, and then again, a little louder. "Hey!"

Sophie turned to see a janitor motioning from a supply closet down the hall. "C'mon. Gotta be quick, or I'm gonna close this back up!" Sophie looked at Aaron, who shrugged. The sound of students jostling and laughing rolled toward them. Lockers slammed and banged. Aaron grabbed Sophie's hand and pulled her through the cracked door, which shut behind them as a wave of noise crashed through the hallway.

CHAPTER SEVENTEEN
LAKE MCLEAN

YODELAYHEEHOOYODELAYHEEHOOYODELAYYODELAY
— HEEHOO

I left before the bell and waited at the edge of the parking lot where the buses lined up, watching teachers and parents walk by. Watching them stare and pretending not to. They all wanted to know, and they were all afraid to ask.

What did it feel like?

I close my eyes and I'm up in the air again, as high as the bleachers. Football players mill below. The band is booming, a big bass drum counting time. Two-two three. Three-two three. The air is crisp and cold. Leaves crunch under booted feet. Two boys are throwing a Frisbee. Parents sip coffee and cocoa and whisky. The sky is a deep fall blue, gnarled clouds looming. I raise my arms, raise one leg, complete a routine. Every routine is the same, a variant of: *Our team is good, your team is bad, we're gonna win if we try super hard.* I'm smiling serious kilowattage, being held by male cheerleader Raffy, who stands on the shoulders of male cheerleader Justin, who stands on the shoulders of a pyramid of Kirstys. It's like being on the prow of a ship. It's like being at the railing of an observation deck.

And then there's the slightest tremble. Keep smiling. There's a sickening wave. Keep smiling. There's no longer anything gripping my thigh, no hand, no support, no innocent squeeze. It's almost like I'm weightless for a full second, just aloft. Isn't *aloft* a funny word? It sounds sleepy. And comforting. And then I am un-aloft. *Bam.* The doctor comes running. The ambulance comes running. The nurse comes running.

The thing is, and it's embarrassing to admit, Zac Grace was my boyfriend freshman year. We'd hang out at his parents' house every weekend, a brick-and-ivy Colonial, and we'd fly to Vail on ski junkets, and we'd fly to Hawaii on volcano-hiking junkets, and we'd drive around in their yellow Range Rover. His parents, with no apparent irony, were named Chad and Tinky. Well, I don't believe it immodest to say that Chad and Tinky loved me. I was part of the family. Until the day I wasn't. *Sorry, no more Vail, hon. Give us a jingle when you get this regenerative-tissue mess cleared up. In the meantime, ciao!*

Which was ironic, since I once asked Chad where all the lucre came from.

"Biotech, hon. Stocks. We own parts of a few companies. A start-up or two."

"Or three," Tinky laughed. "We're a big part of the town renewal."

Chad shushed her and poured another martini.

"See, the rich and the infirm just don't mix," Daddy said after they dumped me, when I was busy crying with my head on his lap. He'd just been fired from his security guard job. Some supervisor he didn't get along with. I tried to laugh but didn't. He tried to laugh but didn't.

Zac was the first person I knocked boots with. I mean for real. In a bed, like a movie, looking in each other's eyes. Also, the last one. His parents were always jetting to Basel or Stuttgart or Cannes, giving us the run of the vacation home. Chad and Tinky out having dinner with Salman Rushdie or Sean Penn or Prince Somebody, while Zac and I are lying on a vicuña couch that overlooks the Matterhorn. Where do you go from there? How do you say no, thank you to glasses of champagne and six-thousand thread-count sheets?

Judge me if you must, but I'm glad. *Life Is Short* is a Hallmark poster, but it's also true. People are always falling out of planes or being run over by Jet Skis or being diagnosed with Ebola, so why wait? I just wish it was someone less blatantly a tool than Zac. True personalities surface when things get difficult or even just inconvenient. As it turns out, Zac has no personality to surface. He has a jump shot. And a yellow car to match his yellow haircut and yellow Dikes. The only thing he really has to offer the world are baby-in-a-blender jokes and hallway fondling. But as long as we're being honest here, I did sort of like the fringe benefits. Deep down, I knew exactly what Zac was, but how many times have you flown to Europe in a Lear? I spent that time spending his parents' money.

Thank gosh something happened to snap me out of it. Thank gosh I started to see things as they really are. Daddy knew all along but was too cool to give me a hard time. Or call me shallow. On the other hand, sometimes I wish Daddy was a little less nice. Daddy being sort of a prick now and again might really come in handy.

"You ready?" he said as the van pulled up in front of the cafeteria.

"Completely."

"Good." He scratched his sideburns. "We have a lot of work to do."

The bell rang. School buses were starting to arrive, parking in long rows. Daddy lowered the gate and strapped my chair in before pulling away from the curb with a chirp.

CHAPTER SIXTEEN
SOPHIE BLUE
AND LARRY

PAST GLORY IS PROLIX GLORY

Aaron let go of my hand as we stepped into the darkness. I almost tripped over a broom. Aaron banged his head against some spray bottles hanging from hooks. "Is this the room you were talking about?"

"Quiet," the janitor whispered, ducking his head. He was a huge slope-shouldered guy with thick glasses. "Gotta wait a minute. Make sure no one saw us."

When a few minutes had gone by and no one knocked on the door, just the usual yelling that swept through the hallway, the janitor said, "S'probably okay now." He inserted a rusty pry-bar into a seam in the wood. There was a whispery creak, and the back wall pushed away. The second room was a little larger, with higher ceilings, but still snug. It had a cot and a heater and a coffeemaker. There was a small TV showing a basketball game, and a desk with some books and papers on it. It was warm and comfy. On the wall there was a poster of 1980s Danny Ainge slamming a basketball in some guy's face. Underneath, it said *No Stopping Chocolate Thunder.*

"You guys can sit over there," the janitor said, pointing to the cot. He unfolded a rusty lawn chair that was leaning against the wall and folded himself back into it. He had weird orangey hair that sat in big curls.

"Wow," I said. "This is . . . wild."

The janitor nodded, pointing to the name in cursive sewed

above his breast pocket, *Larry, Head of Maintenance*. "Name's Larry. I don't really know why I asked you in here. Guess it looked like you needed a minute to get your breath."

"I know what you mean, Larry," Aaron, said, reaching out and holding my hand again. "I mean, in terms of why I'm here. And not knowing. Exactly why. I'm here."

I'd been fantasizing for a year about various scenarios in which Aaron might end up holding my hand, and I still had the urge to pull away. Why? Why did I have to force myself to relax, to just let my hand sit there and accept being held? *You don't need to run*, I told myself. *Unless it's running toward something for once.*

"Coffee?"

Larry pulled the pot from a hot plate. Even though we both shook our heads, he poured three mugs. "You're on the basketball team," he said, blowing steam toward Aaron. His teeth were coffee stained. It was like he was embarrassed about it, trying to keep them closed as much as possible, which gave him a weird way of talking. Pursed, like a fish.

"Yeah, for now," Aaron admitted.

"Used to play a bit of ball myself," Larry said. "You know, a million years ago."

"You went to Upheare?"

"Sure did," Larry said. "Some of them trophies in the hallway cases? They're mine. Or was."

"Go, Toros," Aaron said.

"Go, Toros," Larry said, and they bumped knuckles.

"Larry?" I asked. "Is there — *was* there ever an office across the hallway? A counselor's office?"

Larry chewed a cookie thoughtfully, crumbs falling to the side because he wouldn't open his lips up enough to let it all the way in. "No, ma'am. Behind that wall is pipes, mostly. No room for an office, counselor or otherwise."

"What exactly are you two talking about?" Aaron asked.

"Nothing," I said. "I guess I'm just being paranoid."

Larry held out one finger. "Paranoia will get you through times of no enemies better than enemies will get you through times of no paranoia."

I smiled, tempted to write it down. I was tempted to get it tattooed across my back. Instead, I stuck out my hand and Larry and I bumped knuckles.

"You got anything to read?" Larry asked. "I get real bored. Any magazines or whatever in your book bag?"

"Magazines?"

He sipped his coffee. "Or whatever. Comics. Sometimes people leave them behind. Or sometimes, you know, they get confiscated."

"How long have you been working here, Larry?" I asked.

He held up one finger as a pager went off on his belt. He pressed a few buttons and sighed. "Looks like vomit near the library again. Can y'all explain why no one makes it to the porcelain anymore? What's so great about the rug outside the library?"

"Maybe it's like a dog marking its territory," I said. "The anorexic Kirstys warning the bulimic Kirstys."

"Anyway, you two are gonna have to go now," Larry said. "This room here, as you've probably guessed, is not entirely kosher."

There was still a period left before Trish was due to pick Lake and Kenny and me up.

"It's okay, we need to go to the library anyhow."

"We do?" Aaron said.

CHAPTER FIFTEEN
SOPHIE AND AARON

OBVIOUS IS AS OBVIOUS DOES

We walked to the main desk and I asked the librarian for a reel of microfiche containing the last fifty years of *The Crossly Press-Democrat*.

"What's microfiche?" Aaron asked.

Sitting in front of the huge metal projector, we got online and crossed dates with searches for Sophie Blue, Albert Blue, Fade Labs, Local Experiments, and Menacing Ice Cream Vehicles. I'd already read all the articles about my father disappearing, interviews with detectives who knew nothing and gave the same tired quotes about "working the case" and "hoping someone from the community steps forward." What I'd never done is look for articles that led up to it.

"What is that going to show us?"

"Okay, you know about my father, right?"

Aaron examined his sneaker tops.

"Yeah, yeah," I said. "The rumor, the test tube, I'm an anarchist, I'm the head of a Masonic lodge, I drink the blood of virgins. You don't need to pretend."

"Sure," he said. "Of course I know —"

"You don't," I said. "Trust me."

"Sorry, I —"

"And don't keep apologizing."

He nodded while the computer clicked. Eventually, the search engine responded with just under twelve million hits. I tied the searches together, refining, cross-referencing, and managed to narrow it down to a couple hundred. There were at least twenty articles on the microfiche that corresponded with those hits. Aaron fed the film into the machine, and we began to pull them up, sliding through page after page.

Jan. 19, 1956
Parker-Fade Marriage
Rosemary Emelienko to wed Ben Fade in local ceremony. Prominent young chemistry student Ben Fade marries Ukrainian beauty after graduating magna cum laude from . . .

Mar. 03, 1958
Ben Fade Opens Lab with Local Partners
Local boy Ben Fade has purchased the old Sir Melty's Finest ice-cream factory at the edge of town and is having it refitted as a modern laboratory. "I always knew I wanted to come home and set up a business," he said glowingly to this reporter. "After a number of years overseas working as a contractor for Soviet labs, I decided the time was ripe. Especially since my wife, a registered nurse . . ."

Dec. 10, 1960
Massive Power Outage Cripples Half of State, Fade Labs and Other Local Businesses Report Complete Systemic Failure

Power company officials are at a loss to explain a rare "cascade effect" reaction that blew transformers and seized power stations over a four-hundred-mile radius. Residents are expected to be without power for another week as workmen scramble to effect repairs. "I've never seen anything like it," said James Osterman, a company spokesman. "The kind of juice that was drawn off the grid could have lit up all of Russia. There isn't anything around here I know of requires that kind of power. Not even close."

Dec. 13, 1960
Ben Fade Reported Dead in Tragic Lab Accident

Hundreds turned out to mourn one of the community's bright lights as Ben Fade was buried today after a tragic laboratory accident still under investigation. Firemen called to the scene say the mysterious explosion, which seems to have originated in a room full of machinery known as computers, caused massive damage to the structure and will require . . .

Feb. 17, 1970
Lab Still Sits Empty, Lot Popular
With Vandals
Real estate agent Sydney Barrett says, "It's a crying shame," but they have been unable to find a buyer for the old laboratory all these years, which, although covered with graffiti and barely possessing a window that remains unbroken, still has . . .

June 12, 1988
Fade Labs to Keep Name,
Reopen with New Partners as
BioTech Start-up
Amazingly, Fade Labs is finally back in business, and right there on the cutting edge. A trio of overseas investors have signed papers on the land and begun a massive rebuilding project. The reconstruction of the lab is expected to provide dozens of new jobs for local workers and the entire town seems to have swung behind the effort. From the zoning commission to the Rotary Club, folks are pitching in . . .

Nov. 04, 1989
Groups of Local Men Hired as
Security Guards at Fade Labs
Fade Labs has delivered on yet another promise: to hire directly from the community, picking from numbers of local men

with longtime town standing and, in particular, former Upheare High graduates, when rounding out their new security team. Fresh uniforms have recently arrived and were being fitted as we go to press. "Awesome," said dapper new hire Herbert . . .

Aug. 17, 1990
Odd Number of Missing Person Reports Keeping Local Cops Busy

According to police reports there has been a surge of missing reports in the surrounding area. While most reports are dismissed by police as the result of domestic difficulties, transients, or runaways and there is no evidence of any foul play, the spike in numbers is troubling enough that extra patrols have been added along the waterfront and in industrial sections of town, including the open lots near Fade Labs . . .

Nov. 20, 1992
Autism Cure at Lab Being Tested — Fade Labs Throwing Lot Behind New Experimental Inoculation

Even skeptics in the scientific world are cautiously excited about a possible breakthrough in autism research and a new inoculation that is now being tested at Fade Labs. The local concern recently received the okay to conduct animal trials of their product Bio-Rite, which is being marketed as the first wave of "injectable software," or "bioware." Said a Fade Labs spokeswoman, "Obviously, with considerable industry competition, we can't be too specific until our patent is processed, but Bio-Rite is a new direction in medicine, a software program that interacts with the brain and essentially rewrites . . ."

May 01, 1993
Town Council Votes 8-0 to Invest Pension Fund and Other Available Monies in Fade Labs' Bio Rite II

"We just feel like it's a great investment," said Chester Burnett, town manager. "Given the contracts they've recently been awarded and being so obviously on the scientific cutting edge as well as the dotcom boom, it just seems like a no-brainer that they are a superior investment compared to the volatility of the stock market as a whole. We just thought this was a wiser way to spend our . . ."

Sept. 15, 1994
Volunteers Line Up to Do Their Part with Bio-Rite III

"It's so safe, I'm having my own kids participate," said Albert Blue, standing in front of a group of excited volunteers. "This is a great day, where the notion of community service meets the dictates of responsible science. We here at Fade, White, Templeton, and Sour could not be more proud to be part of this effort to find a cure for autism. And yes, volunteers will receive a small stipend."

(See inset photograph)

"We just want to do our part to help find a cure, or at least a cause, for this tragic disorder," said Donny Ballar, holding the shoulder of his young son, Bryce, and Bryce's best friend, Zac Grace. With him was carpenter Jake Agar and son, Upheare Toros' coach Ron Dhushbak, Winnie Daynes and her daughter, Dayna, with friends Kirsty Crash, Kirsty Cervenka, Kirsty Ving, and Kirsty Morganfield, as well as high school teacher Sadie Last and Albert Blue's two children, Sophie and her younger brother, Kenny.

"Holy crap. That's me!" Aaron said, practically jumping out of his chair.

"Shhh," said the librarian.

"Maybe it's not just my last birthday," I said. "Maybe it's been my last ten birthdays."

"Today's your birthday?" he said. "Happy —"

"Quiet," I shushed. "There's a couple more."

June 10, 1995
Profits from Fade Labs to Fund Town Pool

Ground was broken today on the old Dolphy Farms location, which will soon house the new town pool. Representatives from Fade, White, Templeton, and Sour as well as local officials participated in a ribbon-cutting ceremony in front of construction crews. Smiles abounded as this long-stalled project finally began. Other joint Fade/town projects are on the docket, including many product distribution, retail, and employment concepts being floated by forward-thinking Fade management. "Snap up your retail space now," said lab spokesman Elenora Fagan, "the time for investment is ripe."

May 01, 1996
Popsicle Truck Stolen from Local Man — Teen Prank Suspected

"It's funny," said the truck's owner, Dave "Dubbsy" Thomas, as he stood in his driveway. Thomas, a fixture in local neighborhoods a generation ago with his gleaming white truck and nickel Popsicles, was perplexed. "It didn't even run. The tires were flat. I didn't bother to lock it. I got no clue how they even moved it out of here. . . ."

I hit the cancel button and stopped the flow of articles. Aaron
nodded. "Sorry, I —"

"If you say you're sorry one more time, I swear —"

"Okay, okay," he laughed, putting his hand on my shoulder. I
could feel the calluses on his palm. They were sexy calluses. He
took the dial and spun it back to the picture of the group of volunteers standing outside the laboratory. In the grainy picture,
my father was wearing a lab coat over a white shirt. He had a
huge cheapo watch on his skinny wrist and a bunch of pens in
his front pocket. So did all the other men. Except the four in the
front row, who all wore black suits, presumably the "foreign investors." And there was a woman, standing slightly farther back.
A woman with long legs and a severe mouth, who almost looked
to be wearing a nurse's uniform. Aaron zoomed in, the pixels
widening and abstracting.

"Look how close the Fade chick is. Standing to your father."

It was hard to tell, but it did look like The Nurse was leaning
into him. She had a certain smirk. And my father seemed dis-
tracted, trying to hold it together for the lens. In the very front

was a picture of tiny me in a little skirt and blouse, holding a pocketbook way too big, with a frown on my face.

"That's you, all right. I'd recognize that frown. Anywhere."

"Even without the black lipstick?"

"Especially without. And that's me." Aaron zoomed in. The pixels became huge and grainy. He read aloud: "The widow of Ben Fade has been hired as a laboratory nurse and will be on hand to administer the tests herself. 'After Ben's tragic death, I just wanted to stay involved in his vision in any way I could.'"

I looked closer at the picture. "I totally don't remember any of this. Do you?"

"Not really," Aaron said. "A little, I guess. My dad is big into volunteering. But I had no idea. About your father running things."

Under a separate inset of me was a caption, "Brave Little Volunteer."

"Is *that* why they call you Test Tube?" he whispered. "The real reason?"

I reached over and grabbed his arm.

"What are you —?"

I yanked his sleeve up, but there was nothing on his elbow, no red mark. I tried the other one. Nothing there, either.

"Never mind," I said. "It was just a guess."

I zoomed in to the edge of the photo. A tall man in a security uniform stood with great slumping shoulders. He looked younger but familiar. Very familiar.

"Oh, my God," I said. He was wearing a hat but no glasses. His hair was darker and unpermed. But it was definitely him.

"What?"

In the text under the photo it said, "Larry Goethe, security team recruit."

The screen went blurry. I heard a rush of water in my ears, the nausea starting to rise.

I leaned over, whispering. "We so totally need to get out . . ."

". . . of here?" Larry finished, standing behind us in the little cubicle. He had his mouth wide open now, a big smile, that high brown watermark running across his teeth. He pressed himself against my back and squeezed my shoulders. On the wall behind him was a poster. It had a picture of a smiling dictionary with horn-rimmed glasses. Underneath, it said *Stealing library books is like boning your mom*. I closed my eyes and shook my head. When I opened them, the poster was still there, but it said *Stealing library books is no fun!*

"Sorry," Larry said. "Just thought I'd check up on y'all."

"Hey, thanks," I said, swallowing hard and reaching to the side, blindly trying to turn off the microfiche machine.

"Whacha lookin' at?" Larry smiled.

"Nothing," Aaron said as I found the switch and the screen went dark. "Just checking out some. Sports scores."

"Right," Larry said. "Anyway, I'd like to chat all night, but I've already called in all my favors. It's time to lock up."

"What do you mean?" I asked, wanting to just get up and run. I forced myself to sit still.

Larry looked at his watch. "It's four-thirty. We're the only ones left. Everyone else has gone home."

"We've been in here almost two hours?" I said, shivering. "I was supposed to meet my mother and Lake!"

"And I'm supposed to be at basketball practice."

"Sorry, y'all." Larry smiled, pressing himself closer. I could feel his belt buckle between my shoulder blades. "I would have said something, but I thought you guys wanted some privacy."

Gross, gross, gross.

"Well, hey!" Larry said. "I have a car. I'd be happy to give you guys a ride. Pretty much anywhere."

"Really?" I said, trying to sound enthusiastic.

"Sure thing," Larry said, his orangey hair glinting in the fluorescent light.

I got up and grabbed Aaron's hand, squeezing by. The library was dark. The doors were closed. I didn't hear any teachers talking, or kids. It was completely quiet. "We'll meet you in the parking lot in ten minutes, okay?"

"You sure you don't want to come this way, honeypot?" Larry pointed his thumb toward the closest door, his teeth looking like they'd been steeped in turd water.

"We have to go to our lockers first," I said.

"I don't need to —" Aaron began, but I yanked his arm and pulled him down the hallway.

CHAPTER FOURTEEN
O.S. "KENNY" BLUE

A LITTLE HEART-TO-HEART-TO-HEART

Okay, I waited by the buses for almost an hour? No Sophie. No Lake. No Trish. I looked around in the halls and caf, but they weren't there, either. I finally saw Miss Last, loaded down with a huge pocketbook and an even huger bag of term papers to correct.

"C'mon, Kenny," she sighed. "Help me carry this and I'll give you a ride."

When I got home, was Sophie there? No. I looked up Lake's number in the phone book, but was there an answer? No. In the kitchen, I made four sandwiches and put them on a tray. I added a bag of chips, an apple, two bananas, a spoonful of peanut butter, two yogurts, and then went down to my room and kicked stuff around for ten minutes before I found *Suck Me Twice #12, The Vampire Totally Rises* under a pile of junk. Oh, man, did my room need a quick sweep. On the other hand, I didn't feel like looking for a broom. And was scared of what I'd find if I did, since it looked like the house had been broken into again. I could swear I hadn't left my stack of *Gobble Gobble Gobbler: Cock of the Roost #1–81* against the far wall, and yet, there they were. It was so disturbing that I lay down on the bed and read for a while.

An hour later, after vampire hunter Gunter X had staked about twenty nubile undead, there was still no Sophie. Still no answer at Lake's. Upstairs, I could hear Trish's slippers chuffing across the ceiling. I got up and knocked on her door. There was no answer. I knocked again. There was no answer. I knocked once more.

"*What?*"

"Mom? It's me, Kenny. Is it okay to talk for a minute?"

"Thank you for calling. I'm sorry, but Trish is gone for the evening. Please leave a message after the tone, or try again tomorrow. Beep."

"That would only work if I were on the phone. Mom. Here I am, in person. Open up. Please?"

Trish cracked the door in a pink robe. Her hair stood in pointy shanks. She exhaled. Her breath smelled like freezer burn.

"What is it, honey?"

"You were supposed to pick us up," I said. "At school? And take us to the lab?"

She looked at me blankly. Once when I was ten, she'd picked me up at chess club so red-eyed her head seemed to be floating above her neck, tethered by a string. The teacher, a Russian named Kaprik who favored rapid exchanges, spent the next year asking me if "Everytink was hoky-dory at home."

"It's Sophie," I said. "I think something's wrong."

"More detentions?"

"No. See, this sort of uncomfortable thing happened in the cafeteria, and . . ."

Trish turned away from the door. She went and lay on the bed. I sat on the far corner as she nestled back under the comforters. The room was arctic, the air-conditioning on high. I picked up her *TV Guide,* which had a bunch of shows circled in red.

"This is what you watch?"

"So?"

I read the first name aloud.

"*BloodScene: The Crime Intuiter.*"

"That's a good one," Trish said. "He wears rubber gloves and spots stuff other people missed."

I threw the *TV Guide* on the floor. "So, did you hear what I said?"

Trish covered her face. "I'm tired. You know how sometimes you're so tired, even your bones ache?"

"Um, not really. Listen, can we get in the car and drive around and look for Sophie? I think she's really upset. As you may have noticed, she's been acting a little erratically lately, and . . ."

Trish laughed. The TV laughed with her.

"Okay, erratic for a while now? I'd go look for her myself, but I'm still unlicensed to drive. You promised to fill out my permit paperwork a year ago?"

Trish covered her face. "I've been waiting for this."

"Waiting for what?"

"It changed your metabolism. You were never heavy as a child."

"Huh?"

"He swore there would be no side effects."

"What are you talking about, Mom?"

"Your arm? Does it itch?"

I looked down. The moon-shaped scar at the crook of my elbow not only itched, it throbbed.

"Mom, this is starting to freak me out. Should we maybe even call the police? Or should maybe you, since I'm a minor?"

"You'll be eighteen soon enough," Trish said, the back of her wrist against her forehead, staring at the ceiling. I wondered if she'd finally completely lost it. I wondered if I'd have to call an ambulance. I wondered if I'd have to go into foster care. I wondered what Destruktor-Bot would do.

The phone rang. I picked it up. A man with a deep voice said, "Put your mother on the line, fatty."

I looked at the receiver for a minute.

"Just do it," the booming voice said. I handed it to Trish, who held it away from her ear.

"Yes?"

"Officer Goethe here."

Trish laughed. "Oh, it's you, is it?"

"I've got some business to handle, and then I'm coming over."

"You'll do no such thing."

"I'll be right there," he said, and hung up.

CHAPTER THIRTEEN
SOPHIE AND AARON

GIMME A CHEROOT AND A .22 DERRINGER, AND I'M STRAIGHT

We lay on the grassy hill overlooking the senior parking lot. All the buses were gone, all the students gone. No sign of Lake or Trish or O.S.

"Maybe he really does. Just want to give us a ride," Aaron whispered.

Below us, Larry was walking around his sedan, doing something to the locks in the backseat. Then he rearranged what looked like rolls of duct tape in the trunk.

"Yeah, it's just a coincidence he's pretending to be a janitor," I whispered, pretending not to be terrified. "Maybe later on he's going to make duct tape animals for the kids at the children's hospital."

Aaron's eyes closed to slits. The freckles at his temples faded into his hairline.

"You think I'm just being paranoid," I said.

Aaron shook his head nervously. "That's not true." He put his hand on the small of my back, sneaking it up between my jeans and the bottom of my shirt like he knew things had gotten too weird not to go for broke. And he was right. His hand was warm and reassuring. As a reward, I leaned over and kissed him. His lips were soft and dry. He seemed shocked at first and then kissed me back, pushing too hard. We clanked teeth.

"I don't think you're paranoid at all," he said, rubbing his lip.

"You've got more reason to wig out. Than anyone I know. But you say this crazy stuff sometimes, like, for effect. And you expect people to just accept it, without bothering to explain."

I wanted to be annoyed, but he was right. I didn't have any answers, just a huge duffel bag full of questions.

"How do you know what I expect?" I finally said.

"I've been watching you. Remember? I've seen you in action."

"Watching me?" I said, pulling him by the neck. "You perv. Maybe you're more like Larry that I thought."

He looked horrified, so I kissed him again. I couldn't believe it. Not Aaron and Kirsty Verlaine. Not Aaron and Kirsty Branca. Him and me. I so totally wished Lake could see. She'd never believe it.

Aaron pulled back, catching his breath. "I still don't understand why he'd take the time. To pretend. Being a janitor. I mean, how would he get into the school? Wouldn't people notice? This huge guy standing around?"

His fingers were splayed across my stomach. It was hard to think. His pinkie was in my belly button.

"Yes. No. I mean, to get something from me, is why."

"Get what?"

"It's going to sound stupid."

"We're on a hill. Looking down at some dude with orange hair. Ready to chauffeur us. To a place where you need a whole lot of duct tape. I think you can probably go ahead and say it."

"A comic book."

Aaron laughed. Larry looked up, and we ducked our heads. I counted to ten and then peeked out again. Larry was looking at his watch, tapping his foot.

"It's not funny," I whispered. "Our house has been broken into at least six times in the last year. I'd bet anything Larry, I mean Officer Goethe, was the one who did it. They've been looking for something. And I think that's what they've been looking for."

Aaron seemed concerned, but I couldn't tell if it was about the break-ins or my mental health. "So now what?"

"We don't go anywhere with Janitor Clown Wig. We need to find another way to the lab."

"As in your father's lab? Isn't it all closed up?"

I was two inches from Aaron's face. The stubble on his chin had chafed my cheeks. No matter what I said, he probably wasn't going to believe me. He was on the team. Zac Grace was his best friend. That was enough to get out of any jam, win a couple of trophies and you're immune to the world.

"Are you sure you don't want to go to practice? Maybe you should just go."

He shook his head. "I'll get reamed by Coach Dhushbak. Either way. I might as well take my medicine tomorrow."

"If there's a tomorrow."

"Okay, Sunshine," he laughed. Beneath us, Officer Goethe slammed his car door and jogged back into school.

"He's going in to look for us," I said. "Now's our chance."

We did a sort of Navy Seal crouch down the hillside until we were alongside the sedan. There was no way Larry would have been dumb enough to leave the keys in the ignition, was there?

There wasn't.

"We're walking?" Aaron said. "The lab is, like, miles. From here."

"Then we better get started," I said, keeping my head low as we ducked between cars and ran toward the main road. "Especially since we need to make a quick stop first."

An hour later, we were standing on a cement island in a busy two-lane street.

"We're never going to get there," Aaron said.

It was hot and we were both sweating. We'd barely made it halfway to the center of town, mostly because of all the time we spent hiding behind trees when anything that looked like Larry's sedan was coming.

"It's true," I said. "It's time for drastic measures."

"It is?"

I crossed my arms and stood in a way I thought seemed worldly. "I keep asking myself, if there are no rules, why am I playing by the rules?"

"That's a bumper sticker," he said. "What does it mean?"

I'd been thinking about it during the walk. Maybe I was crazy, maybe not. Maybe the vacuum store really did exist, or maybe I was just here, in an even more believable scenario, holding Aaron's hand while we ran from an evil janitor. Either way, why was I going with the program? Write me an essay, go to detention, sit up in your room and be scared and just take it. Take it in school, take it from Trish, take it from Dad. Sit there and draw like a good little girl and pretend nothing's wrong.

Well, something *was* wrong. Really wrong. I'd spent an entire year waiting around for someone else to show up and make it right. If I wasn't crazy, I was at least justified to act like I was. And if I *was* crazy, it didn't matter what I did, because it was all in my head. I'd had a free pass all along.

"Stay here," I said.

I walked across the street, looking for a convenience store, but came to a bank first. The guard smiled and held the door for me. He was young and cute. I slapped his face. Not very hard, but hard enough. As he held his cheek, I slid the gun from his holster, which was Western and elaborately tooled. I motioned to the floor.

"Safety's on," he said.

"No, it isn't," I said, and squeezed the trigger, guessing right. The gun fired a shot into the far wall. Everyone froze. The barrel snapped back and nearly clonked me in the head. I motioned to the floor again, my hands vibrating, and this time the guard got into a crouch.

"Sorry," I whispered as he lay facedown. "Total emergency."

The teller was a woman with a tight bun.

"Money," I told her loudly. "Put all the cash in your drawer into a bag, don't press anything, don't do anything, no dye packs or alarms or fake bills." It was a speech straight out of every heist movie. I swept the gun in a wide arc and fired a few rounds into the ceiling. My ears rang. People screamed. Some lady moaned. Her necklace broke, and dozens of pearls rolled across the floor. The teller pushed a plastic bag toward me.

I grabbed a huge handful of bills and threw them in the air.

"Quick, everybody, take it before the police get here!"

As some people started to gather the bills, I stepped over the security guard and whispered, "You're sorta cute. You should have asked for my phone number."

A block away, sirens went off. I walked back to where Aaron was standing, looking pissed and confused at the same time. He pointed at the bag.

"Please tell me you didn't just do. What I totally think you just did."

"We can afford a cab now," I said.

"Listen to me," he said. "No matter what's wrong, we can . . ."

I saw something glinting over his shoulder. "Wait here again."

Across the street, Coach Dhushbak was sitting in his convertible, finishing dinner. He tossed an empty Sour White onto the curb, tightened his mesh driving gloves, and zipped up his red leather jacket. Sunglasses were perched on the top of his head. He looked at me, licked his lips, and burped.

"Gothika? Why aren't you in school?"

"School's over," I said.

He frowned and popped up his collar. "You want a ride? Hop in. We'll go straight to detention."

"I do want a ride," I said. "Just not with you."

"Excuse me?"

"Get out. I'm driving."

"No way." Coach Dhushbak laughed. "No one drives my car. Especially not a —"

I leveled the gun at his hairline. The sirens were really going off now.

"Keys," I said.

I pulled a U-turn, gunned it down the street, and chirped up to the curb, where Aaron was practically growing a bald spot. "Need a ride, sailor?"

He looked at the bag of money in back, which had opened and spilled everywhere, and then at me. I revved the engine.

"I don't understand. Weren't we just —?"

"I'll explain on the way," I said. "Hop in."

"Not like this. Not unless you —"

I put the car in gear. "Unless I what? Didn't you see your picture in that article, too?"

"Yeah, I saw it," he said. "I just thought I was. Getting to know you."

"You don't know me at all."

His eyes looked hurt. I pointed to my chest with the gun, and he winced.

"What you like today will probably be different tomorrow. Or in five minutes. It's all just a stupid game. Spin the wheel, win a prize. Except there is no prize."

"That's the lipstick talking," he said. "The role you play. Scare everyone at school so you don't have to take a chance on getting too close."

I stared at him. His resigned face and almond-shaped eyes. I shouldn't have brought him this far. Then again, he shouldn't have wanted to come.

"You can get in or not."

He looked back at the bank, where the police were now in crouching positions behind fenders and car doors, pointing their guns at the big plateglass window and telling people to come out with their arms up. The security guard was trying to explain something, but they weren't listening. Coach Dhushbak was yelling and waving his arms and pointing at us, until one of the cops stood and cuffed him.

Aaron slid in beside me.

"To be honest?" I said. "I didn't think you were going to —"

"Shut up and drive," he said.

I stomped the gas. The red convertible roared down Main Street. We needed to get on the highway, but I wasn't sure where the entrance was.

"Cops," Aaron said, craning his neck. "Behind us."

Sirens twirled. Two cruisers pulled into chase formation. I slowed down, signaling like I was going to pull over.

"Thank God," Aaron said, opening the glove compartment to look for the registration. Instead, he pulled out a handful of porno mags.

"That's Dhushbak," I said, and tossed the magazines in the air, one of them centerfolding onto the cop's windshield with a breasty slap, causing him to nail a stop sign. Aaron gripped the dashboard. We zoomed by some enormous guy jogging on the side of the road who sort of looked like Kenny. I almost laughed. Kenny. Jogging.

"Please stop," Aaron said.

"We need some music," I said, flipping the dial until I found a radio station playing "In the Hallway" by Perv Idols. *"I saw you by locker numbah twelve, so hot, so right, so fine tonight, but baby baby baby, do you know my com-bi-na-tion . . . ?"*

The sirens closed in as we came to a long straightaway. The wind howled in my ears. We were up over a hundred, the horizon and the sky beginning to blur. We caught a little air over a rise, the music jangling.

"Oh, no."

"After all this, there's an oh, no?"

"Hold my hand," I said.

Aaron shrugged. Our fingers entwined.

"Maybe we'll get lucky," I said, flooring it even harder. "Maybe we'll spin the big wheel and land on Brad and Angelina."

Aaron nodded, with complete acceptance of my insanity. "I'm not that into adoption."

A hundred ten. A hundred twenty.

The Popsicle Man's grill loomed, glinting in the sun, before slamming into us with a long, broken, tearing sound, completely, utterly, and directly head-on.

CHAPTER TWELVE
THE RELUCTANT
LEADER

IT'SONLYADREAM IT'SONLYADREAM
IT'SONLYADREAM. I THINK

Y
ou brought a friend?"

"I guess."

"That's not supposed to happen," Mr. Puglisi said.

"Just let me spin and get it over with," I said, reaching for a can of Sour White as the wheel clicked to a stop. ZOMBIE FREAK-OUT.

"You gotta be kidding me."

I opened my eyes as the first one came shuffling through the senior parking lot. It bumped against a station wagon, bounced off, and stared dumbly at the sun. No one paid much attention, but I knew exactly what it was. The thing approached a pair of sophomore girls smoking by the rear stairwell. It bit the first girl on the arm. The other girl watched, amazed. She might even have laughed. Then the thing bit her, too, and she stopped laughing. I raised my hand. Miss Last pursed her lips, writing on the board with a piece of squeaky chalk. The two girls now lay in the grass. By the time Miss Last wrote *Coriolis* and *Borealis* the girls were shuffling like groupies behind the thing. I stood up.

Miss Last swept back her tinted bangs and released a detention-esque sigh. "*Yes*, Sophie?"

"Um . . . there's a zombie? No, three zombies. Right outside."

Every head in the class turned, but no one said a word. Miss Last did not say a word. Bryce Ballar, for once, did not say a word.

Aaron, at the desk next to me, leaned over and hissed, "What in hell is going on?"

I shrugged, hissing back. "We're, um, dead? On the other hand, maybe not. Maybe you're not here at all. Except you're in most of my other dreams, too."

Aaron rolled his eyes and looked embarrassed, but also sort of pleased. "I'm in your dreams?"

"Pretty much."

He nodded. "Like, do we ever —"

"I think we need to concentrate on what's going on outside."

"Which is what?"

"Not sure yet." I straightened up, addressing the class. "Seriously, if any of you want to live, you'll need to listen to me."

Everyone pressed their faces against the Science Room window and saw the Smoking Girls with their pasty eyes and chunk-bitten arms chunk-biting seniors outside the cafeteria.

Miss Last said, "Oh, shit."

For the first time I realized she probably had a boyfriend and listened to records at night and drank cheap beer while watching sitcoms and couldn't wait for every school day to end, just like everyone else, standing there in her itchy skirt, explaining the difference between Paleolithic and pahoehoe.

"Give me your key ring," I said.

Miss Last stared at me for a moment and then, amazingly, un-hooked it from her belt.

The class moved through the hallway as I instructed, single file and with precision. Somehow I knew zombies hated precision. Near the computer lab a security guard was emptying his revolver into the ceiling, while three toothy jazz-dance girls swarmed his legs. Some freshman was trying to stuff himself into a locker. Principal Whithers was digging his incisors into Kirsty Fripp's calf. He looked up at me with a big, unseeing zombie smile. I shattered a display case with one kick, rooted around inside for something heavy, and brained him.

"Gross," Aaron said.

"Nice swing," Bryce Ballar said.

I dropped the gooey basketball trophy (*Go, Upheare Toros, 1982 Semifinalists!*) and started forward again. The class surged along behind me.

The equipment locker was a steel mesh storage cage welded onto the rafters above the courts. It was stuffed with equipment. Climbing ropes dangled over mats on the gym floor. Once the door was locked and buttressed, I ordered Bryce Ballar (who saluted) to pull the climbing ropes onto the platform. I told Kirsty Rawls to find a pad and pencil and take inventory of the Juicy J Juicer-Boxes and Crunch-a-Chip Mini-Pouches stacked in the corner. I had Kirsty Templeton assign each student a yoga mat, a pommel horse blanket, and a deflated basketball-pillow. Finally, I asked Miss Last to begin fashioning orange highway cones into commodes so the waste could be aimed out the side vent, onto the faculty lounge below. As the class took on tasks and became organized, Aaron came and stood next to me.

"You're really something. Like the girl Bruce Willis."

It was too sarcastic to even respond to.

"Now, Bruce, do you think you could do me a huge favor and tell me what the hell's going on? Who was that guy. With the roulette wheel?"

"It was Mr. Pug —"

There was a pounding at the steel door. Three slams, a pause, three more. Kirsty Westerberg started crying. The air ducts ticked and creaked. The pounding began again. Bryce Ballar picked up a Louisville Slugger 40 oz. Derek Jeter and positioned himself within swinging distance of the knob. I got on my knees and peeped under the door. There was a sliver of light and two feet. Not four, six, or eight feet. Not ten, twelve, or fourteen feet. Just two.

"Who is it?"

"Coach Dhushbak!" came a quavery yell. "Lemme in, I've lost my keys!"

Most of the class sighed. Dhushbak? Jesus. Shorts inspections were next.

"Don't let him in," Kirsty Lords whispered.

"*Hurry!* There's something down there! It's coming up!"

I looked at Miss Last, who shrugged. Dhushbak was a fanny slapper, notorious around the faculty coffee machine.

"Prove you're human."

"That you, Gothika?" Coach Dhushbak almost laughed. "Okay, I'll prove it. You just bought yourself another week of detention."

I sighed and let him in.

For an hour, everyone sat on the floor, eating snack chips and trying not to listen to the smacking and gnawing sounds coming from below. Aaron kept cornering me, but I pretended to be busy organizing. "Either I'm crazy, you're crazy, or we're both crazy. Okay? How's that?"

"I think I've found something," Miss Last called. She'd been rummaging in the back, where some old file cabinets were pushed against the wall. Next to them were big piles of paper arranged in stacks on the floor.

"What is it?"

"Mostly crap," Miss Last said. "Board meeting minutes. Plans for evacuation in case of earthquake. Pay structure and benefits schedules. Except this."

It was a ten-page report outlining an agreement between Fade Labs and the school board. It was signed by Principal Whithers. It was a list of students who had been inoculated in The Nurse's office. The inoculations were provided by Fade Labs. For agreeing to be part of the study, the school had been paid twenty thousand dollars, and a new basketball court had been installed.

"No way."

The list included most of the class, as well as the ones before and after. It was hundreds of students.

"What does it mean?" Aaron said, looking over my shoulder.

"I'm not sure."

"That's not good enough."

"Don't. Aaron?"

He climbed onto a crate of Bonzo-Boy Pork Muncher-Hunks and signaled for everyone's attention. "Listen, I've been thinking about it, and I'm thinking maybe we should go down there."

"Excuse me?" Bryce Ballar wheezed.

"C'mon, haven't you guys ever seen a zombie movie?" Aaron laughed. "Well, I have. I've seen them all. And the one thing I know for sure is zombies don't bite people for food. Zombies aren't hungry. Zombies won't ever be hungry."

"Then what are they?" Kirsty Doe asked.

"They're lonely," Aaron said. "They bite because they want us to be like them. When everyone's like them, they won't have to be embarrassed. Anymore."

Some people began to nod.

"Embarrassed about what?" Miss Last asked.

"About the rotting," Aaron said, staring right at me. "And the smell. And the face-skin dangling. And their inability to talk. About books at parties. Or make fun of the president. In an ironic voice. I mean, what are we really afraid of? Sure, they're ugly, but they don't know they're ugly. Maybe they're just like us."

There was more nodding. Most of the class drifted over to the other side of the cage, standing near Aaron.

"What are you, a frickin' retard?" Ballar said. "A frickin' vegan? They're *eating* people."

Aaron grabbed a case of Oranger-Rella Guzzle Mists under each arm and unlocked the door.

"No!" Bryce Ballar shouted, reaching for his bat, but it was too late. Aaron scampered down the staircase.

An hour later, when Aaron hadn't returned, the rest of the class went down as well. There were hundreds of zombies in the gym. Most of the lights were off. It had just been decorated for prom, a stage and streamers and a big banner. Miss Last found a radio and turned it on loud. Girl zombies stood along one wall, and boy zombies stood along the other. A few paired off and began to dance. They spun, fell, and laughed in their own dim way. A zombie's leg fell off. He picked it up and samba'd with it. The Clash came on, and other zombies did the pogo. The music got louder; the yelling got louder. Finally, even Bryce Ballar said screw it and went down. A cheer echoed, or maybe it was a moan. There was laughing, or maybe screaming. A zombie boy directly below me was wearing a Timberlake's A Puss T-shirt. Coach Dhushbak was curled up in the corner, rocking back and forth and singing to himself.

I could stay or I could go now.

I untied the rope securing the trapdoor, dangling for a moment above the crowd, then lowered myself to the floor. There was a pause in the dancing. The music continued to pound, but the zombies stood, watching me. They bared their teeth, not friendly at all. A few of them had their sleeves pulled up. I could see red marks on their elbows. I couldn't see Aaron, or anyone else from the class. The floor was covered with something wet and slick, but I was afraid to look down. There was a collective roar. It was like being stung by a thousand bees, set to clanging music, teeth and fingers, as a series of backfires came, squealing tires and a frozen grill.

CHAPTER ELEVEN
KENNY "O.S." BLUE

LIKE BO JACKSON, BUT BIGGER, ROUNDER, SLOWER, WHITER, AND SWEATIER

I can handle Goethe," Trish said. "You should go. Quickly."

"Why?" I said. "I don't understand —"

"Just go," she snapped. "Don't you ever listen?"

I looked at my mother, already standing and straightening her hair. I knew it was pointless to argue. Talking to Trish was like picking up a jellyfish and trying to keep it from leaking between your fingers. She looked at me in the mirror and made a shooing motion with her hand. I went to my room and filled my messenger bag with snacks and comics. Was there anywhere for me to go? Not really. Back to school? No. To Johnny Hex's Comics and Collectibles Shoppe? No. Straight to Lake's, pound on the door, and find out what's up? Check.

I clambered down the steps and huffed out the back, hiding behind a tree as a car pulled into the driveway. An ungainly man in a security uniform clomped up the front walk and entered like he'd done so before. Many times before. The door slammed behind him.

Out on the street, car after car after car flashed by, ignoring my thumb. No one was ever going to give me a ride. I considered my options. Since there were none, except lying on the side of the road and eating bag after bag of Cheeze Nobz, I began to jog. With any luck, I'd drop a dozen pounds by the time I got to Lake's house. I hadn't run in a year. Actually, I wasn't really running now. It was more like a wobbly shuffle. Sweat immediately began to sheet down my neck, from my ears, through my scalp. Cars beeped and honked, people leaning out and yelling. The very same cars that had ignored me entirely when I was asking for a ride.

"Hey, Forrest Plump! Where you runnin' to?"

"Hey, Orson Welles! They givin' out free chicken buckets somewhere?"

"Hey, Norbit, you just eat Big Momma *and* the Nutty Professor?"

Oh, man, humanity.

A red convertible whipped by at about a thousand miles an hour, three police cars behind it, but I was too tired to even look up. My knees throbbed, my heart contused. I was soaking wet, my legs felt like tubes filled with ground glass, my pulse was unquantifiable, and there were only thirty-five more blocks to go.

"Hey, Shamu! You lost? The million gallon pool's thataway."

It took four tries to spear the bell. I held it as long as I could and then slumped against the side of the house. Lake's father, the guy I'd seen at the pool, answered the door. When he saw the shape I was in, he grabbed my arm, straining against my sweaty ballast. He finally managed to lever half of O and most of S onto the couch, as Lake covered my head and neck with cold cloths.

"Just take it easy there, big guy," her father kept saying.

The house was filled with cans and wrappers and pieces of machinery and binoculars and hammers and hats and shoelaces and flowerpots and spoons and doll heads and fondue sets. There were paths through it all, which I assumed was to make way for Lake's wheels. On the far wall was a poster. It was a picture of a bearded guy in a robe with his legs crossed, giving the camera the finger. Underneath it said *Om You, Buddy!*

Lake wheeled beside me, while I haltingly told her about Officer Goethe and Trish.

"Thank God you're here, safe," Lake said with an unusually big smile. "That guy sounds freaky."

"I couldn't get you on the phone," I said.

"So you *ran* over?"

"Sort of more like a gentle lope?"

Her father pulled out a huge hunting knife, grabbed a blanket that had a sort of horsey, New Mexico-ish pattern to it, and made a long cut in the center.

"What's that for?"

"Emergency shirt."

He pointed to my sweat-soaked hoodie and gestured to the blanket's slit. I took the hoodie off and slid my neck through the blanket's hole. It settled over me like a poncho, like the one Clint Eastwood wore in *The Good, the Bad and the Ugly.* It was totally, amazingly cool.

He held out his hand. "Hi, I'm Herb."

"O.S.," I said.

We shook.

"So, what does O.S. stand for?"

"Overwhelmingly Studious."

Herb smiled. His mustache twitched.

"You know, I hate to say this?" I said, saying it anyway, "since you guys have been so welcoming, but I —"

"You want to find your sister. You want to go to the lab?"

"Right."

"Don't worry about Sophie," Herb said. "I'm on it."

Lake looked adoringly at her father, and then at me. "Sometimes Daddy'll forget it's a school day and take me to the movies," she said in a monotone. "Or, we'll watch three hours of TV and he'll roll over and say, 'Let's take a break, who wants to watch some TV?'"

"Oh," I said. There was something off about her, like she'd gone kind of slack. I wanted to snap my fingers in her face.

"That's enough, Lake," Herb said.

Lake sort of looked at the ceiling like she hadn't heard him, speaking even more slowly. "Back when I had friends and stuff, Zac and Dayna and Kirsty and Kirsty always wanted to come over. I was like, 'Hey, you guys wanna go to the mall or the beach or the movies?' And they were always like, 'Uh, hey, is Herb home? Let's go to your house and chill with him instead.' Isn't that funny?"

"Hilarious."

"Daddy was always like, 'Hey guys, we should all volunteer.' And everyone was like, 'Yeah, cool idea. But first let's have more cookies.'"

"Do you need a nap, hon?" Herb said. "Maybe you need a nap."

Lake sort of wheeled sideways and stared at the poster on the wall. Her mouth hung open.

"Um, Lake?" I said. She didn't answer. The second or third time, either.

CHAPTER TEN
SOPHIE AND TRISH REDUX

WORDS OF TRUTH AND PASSION

Mr. Puglisi wasn't in the vacuum store. Vacuums weren't in the vacuum store. It was completely empty, like everything had been boxed up and shipped out. There was a broom and piles of dirt and an empty desk. Behind the desk was the big wheel, but all the colored triangles were gone. Except one. It was bright blue. In the center it said SOPHIE. On the floor was a warm can of Sour White, bent in half and almost empty. Underneath it was a note with three words. Just like my progress report. And in the same handwriting.

Pull The Cord.

I looked around the room. There were no cords.

Of any kind.

Anywhere.

The big wheel clackity-clacked around and around and around, landing on the blue triangle, dead center, the very first time.

I was alone, nauseated, and shivering, lying in a hammock in someone's backyard. Across the street, four police cruisers were parked around a red convertible on the side of the road. Policemen stood and gestured, explaining something to one another, none of them entirely convinced. There wasn't a scratch on me, but it still took a minute to get rid of the sensation of zombie fingers. I rubbed my eyes and tried to decide what to do. Staying in the hammock, forever weeping, was one option.

I got up and walked through the yard, into the neighbors', and across two more streets, cutting through gardens and mini putting greens. When I got to our house, I slid open the glass door off the kitchen and tiptoed inside. The television was on, loud. I considered knocking on Trish's door and telling her everything. What did I have to lose? My knuckles hung in midair as a buzzing went off and a studio audience cheered. Trish cheered along with them. I put my hand away.

Kenny's room was an unbelievable mess. I kicked over piles of junk and leafed though bags of stuff in the corners. It was mostly empty bottles of cologne and mismatched socks and food wrappers. His bed was unmade, the sheets and blankets swirled up into one big pile. Under the bed, there were cardboard boxes filled with comics, but none was the one with the robot, mostly hottie vampires and talking carrots and heavily armed lizards croaking at one another to *Attack! Attack!*

Did Kenny hide La Nutrika, or did he always carry it with him? I walked across the hall to the storage room, where Trish had punted the boxes of stuff my father had left behind. I rooted through them, but there were no comics, just horns of aftershave, notes, glass beakers, some clothes, khakis and starched lab coats, framed degrees and cheap watches and pen sets. In the last box was a stack of Polaroids. There were more pictures of the reopening of the lab, construction crews, the cutting of a ribbon. My father standing with his partners. My father standing with Rose Fade. There was also a thick sheaf of letters. I skimmed through them. They started out businesslike, discussing clinical trials and equipment orders, and then became more familiar, a little flirtatious. Finally, at the bottom of the pile was a pink envelope. It smelled like perfume and was written on expensive paper.

Albert,

How could you? After that day in the rhesus room, I was filled with such elation. I'd waited so long to feel again after Ben. Perhaps you do not understand the meaning of the word betrayal, but I do. And you will. There's nothing the world hates more than a thief.

Now that the final procedures are in place for the reopening of the conduit, your little kite had better fly. And then, when you have completed the test run, we will have a long talk. A very long talk.

Best to Wifey,
Rose

I almost swallowed my tongue when I heard the door slam. I was nailed. Trish would come down, see me, see the note, and . . . there were no footsteps. No Trish voice. I realized the slam had been the front door. Moron. I crept to the top stairs to see who it was.

Trish was sitting on the sofa with a glass of wine. She was more made-up than usual, wearing a clean robe, her hair shaped. Officer Goethe stood in front of the fireplace in his security uniform, his legs spread wide. His glasses were gone. His orange perm was gone. He tucked his thumbs into his pockets and grinned.

"Don't stand there like an ape," Trish said. "Find a glass and pour yourself a drink."

"Not now," Goethe said. "I'm here for them both. It's time."

"Finally earning your paycheck, huh, Larry?" Trish said. "Well, neither of them are here. So maybe you shouldn't be, either."

Goethe sighed. "Do I need to look around? Poke in a few drawers?"

"Go ahead," Trish said, and took a big gulp. "You might find some panties your size."

Goethe turned red. He knocked a chair and a table over. He cut open a few pillows with a utility knife. Then he went upstairs and kicked stuff around. There was no way to sneak out without Trish seeing. Would she tell him? And I still didn't have the comic. I couldn't just stay on the stairs and wait to find out. Washing machine? The closet? People were always hiding in air vents in spy movies, but ours was just about big enough to fit a rectangle of Velveeta. When I heard Larry coming back down, I crawled under Kenny's bed. Perfect. Under the bed. No one would ever think to look there. I tossed disgusting-smelling sheets and wet towels over myself, stuffing my legs and butt as far back as they would go. It smelled worse than horrible. Larry's boots clomped into the room. He belched and tossed things around. He broke something. And then something else. It was completely silent for a minute. I fought the temptation to peek. Then he began stabbing his knife into the mattress. The blade nipped all the way through to the underside, just the silvery tip winking at me each time. *Pop pop pop.* I pressed my face against the wall. *Pop pop pop.* I tried not to breath. *Pop pop pop.*

The tip of the knife clipped my knuckle.

Pop pop pop.

I stuck my finger in my mouth and tried not to yell, tasting blood.

Pop pop pop.

The knife tore my skirt, making a different sound than the mattress.

"You in here, fatty?" Goethe called, kicking a chair. I heard him clomp back up the steps. When I was sure it wasn't a trick, I opened my eyes. It was tempting not to move. But the smell had gotten worse, and there was something sweaty and plastic pressed against my face. I twisted halfway out. It was a comic. In a plastic sleeve. A robot with a big steel jaw was staring back at me. Destruktor-Bot. I wrenched myself the rest of the way from the bed and slipped it down the front of my shirt.

Goethe was back on the sofa next to Trish.

"I missed you," he said, finishing her wine.

"Cut the crap," she said, grabbing her glass back.

"Maybe you better come with me," Goethe said.

"I'm not going anywhere with you."

"You *been* somewhere with me," he said, grinning his watermark grin. I tried not to gag. He pulled out a chrome briefcase and spun the lock. Inside was a needle.

"You've got to be kidding," Trish said.

Goethe laughed and pulled up his sleeve. "This isn't from the lab. Private stock. I thought you and me could party."

"You always know just what to bring," she said. "Flowers? Wine? Nothing so crude for a gentleman like you."

"Just the kind of gentleman you like," he said. When he turned to pick up the case, I ducked back through the kitchen and out the sliding glass doors.

CHAPTER NINE
SOPHIE BLUE

WILL THE CONTESTANT STEP RIGHT THIS WAY?

I slipped along the side of the house and ran up the driveway to Officer Goethe's sedan. There was no way he would have been dumb enough to leave the keys in the ignition. Not a chance.

Except there they were, dangly and shiny and gorgeous. I almost laughed out loud. Until I heard the front door open. Larry stood in the doorway, and he was the one doing the laughing.

"Honeypot!" he said. "You're home!"

I gave him the finger, and he stopped smiling.

"You're a dick, Larry," I said. "Fake janitor!"

He ran at me, taking the steps two at a time. I yanked the handle, getting the door open, getting my shirt caught on it, wedging myself into the front seat. Larry kept coming, his huge boots making divots in the lawn. I turned the key and closed the door just as his shoulder crumpled into the side, leaving a massive dent. He pounded the window, first with the flat of his hand, then with his fist. I put the car in gear, reversing quickly to the left. The fender sank into his belly and tossed him like a sock full of pudding. I floored it backward, out of the driveway, *Toot toot, beep beep, talking 'bout bad girls.*

Two streets over, I slowed next to the group of police cruisers. They were still parked, sirens flashing and reflecting off Coach Dhushbak's convertible. I gave the officers a friendly wave and rolled down my window.

"There's a man back there trying to break into that house."

"Excuse me?" the officer said.

"Right back there. A big apey guy with a suitcase full of drugs. Lying on the lawn."

One policeman looked back at the others, and they began to jog across the street, holding their batons against the side of their legs.

"Stay right here," the first one called.

"You bet," I said.

In the parking lot outside the lab was a security booth. I knocked on the window. It was empty. On a hook over a monitor hung a key ring. I grabbed it and slid one of the two keys into the lab's elaborate lock. It fit perfectly. The door wheezed, rusty hinges making tiny little protests.

Inside was a small anteroom of greenish concrete. There was a wrought-iron bench and a dead plant and some papers on the floor. Against the far wall was another smaller door, with a sign that read EXTREME CAUTION. VERBOTEN.

The second key also fit perfectly. I inched the smaller door ajar. Inside, the laboratory was dark and wet. It was filled with offices that looked looted. Walls of computers were smashed. Exposed wires hung from the ceiling and from inside broken components. Random lights blinked, in last-ditch attempts to function. Water vats were cracked or overturned, spilling their contents across the floor. Papers were everywhere, graphs, stacks of numbers, rolls and rolls and rolls of printed code, floating in puddles and impaled on shards of glass.

"Hello?"

There was no answer, but I could see someone seated behind a rusty steel desk. That someone was wearing a dirty nurse's uniform.

"Took you long enough," Rose Fade croaked.

She'd aged thirty years. Or fifty. Her face was lined and her fingers were bent. She was barely able to hold the cane that sat across her lap.

"Have you brought what I asked for?"

I slid *The Adventures of Destruktor-Bot and Manny Solo, Boy Mentor* from my shirt. She reached out, but I pulled the comic back. She almost fell over, steadying herself angrily.

"First, tell me why you want it."

Rose Fade poured herself a glass of water and took a tiny sip, her hand shaking. "I want it, my dear, because it's the only physical item to be taken out of the Virtuality. So far."

"It's just a comic book," I said. "My father gave it to Kenny."

"Your father gave it to Kenny," Rose agreed. "After *you* brought it out yourself. A year ago today. In this very office."

The memory of that day trickled into me like rusty water. The pain. Her fingers gripping my arm, Goethe holding me down. My father watching from the shadows.

"I remember the needle," I said, starting to shake. "I remember having a dream."

"That's right," Rose said soothingly. "Let it all come back."

I held the comic up, staring at the cover. Flashes of being in a soccer uniform, of the injection, of going to the vacuum store and spinning the wheel settled through me. I had a flash of being in an apartment. There was a child in a crib. My husband (husband?) lay on the couch, watching a football game. I sat at an easel, drawing. I was older. An adult. My clothes were spotted with ink. My hair was long, in a ponytail. A large piece of paper was spread before me, broken into panels. I was inking a picture, with careful shading and cross-hatching. My son cried. *My son.* I turned, spilling the ink bottle, a black puddle oozing over drawings of a robot. "Hey," my husband said, kissing my neck. "Careful. There goes this month's rent!"

I was the one who drew *The Adventures of Destruktor-Bot.*

I was trying to tell myself something.

"But that was a dream," I said, closing my eyes, trying to hold on to the memory. It slowly seeped away. I wanted another glimpse of my husband. I wanted another glimpse of my freckled child, but it was gone.

"Haven't you read your own work?" Rose asked. "Ben Fade knew exactly what he was doing. Tangible things *can* be brought from the Virtuality."

I stared at the drawings. My drawings. The Nurse and the robot. And Manny Solo. Like a skinny Kenny. Like my brother before Dad left, but grown-up and sarcastic and heroic. I wanted to hold on to it. And I knew wanting it was dangerous. I needed not to care about anything to do with Rose Fade.

"Maybe I should just tear it up."

"No," she said, rasping. "It's my property. Your father stole it from me."

"I don't believe you," I said, thinking about the last time I'd seen him, rummaging in the basement, frantic. I thought about how I'd just been repeating his steps.

Rose held her arm toward the door. "Fine. So there's the exit. You found your way in, you can find your way out. Don't forget to have the guard validate your parking ticket."

She was right. I had no leverage. What was I going to do? Go back home? Let it start all over again?

"Your father tried to sell our little program on the open market," Rose said softly, "but even multinationals have limits. Internal safeguards, blah. Ethics committees, blah. They weren't interested in buying after the first . . . failures. But they will definitely be buying now."

"Why now?"

"You're holding it. Proof trumps ethics every time."

I stared at her.

"But why believe what I say? Come with me, and you can ask your father yourself."

CHAPTER EIGHT
ROSE FADE

THE ROSETTA STONED

R ose stood and hobbled through a series of dark offices, not looking back to see if I was following. We came to a long metal staircase that wound down the side of a hangarlike room. At the bottom of the staircase was another, smaller lab, this one intact and spotless. It was lit by a series of blue fluorescent tubes highlighting a circle of glass vats. Inside each vat was a dog, floating in some kind of yellowish gel, hooked up to tubes. A sign read Canis Control Group One.

"The first generation," Rose said.

"Twinkle!" I whispered.

"A noble sacrifice," Rose said, pretending to wipe a tear from her eye.

I glared at her, but she just shrugged like, What can you do?

Behind the dogs was another room filled with machinery, and in the center of the machinery was a rectangular pool. Exactly like the town pool. It was a model replica, with a fence and a snack bar. I was about to ask why, when Rose said, "A comfortable and familiar environment means productive workers."

There were people floating, connected to dozens of tubes, on their backs, eyes closed. Just their heads stuck out from the surface. Except it didn't look like water. It was thicker, more viscous.

"Conducting fluid," Rose said. "Also, a secondary nutrition source."

Some of the people had the fluid in their mouths. A couple seemed to be mechanically swallowing.

"No way," I said.

Rose smiled. "Sour White concentrate."

I held a hand over my mouth.

"Pure protein."

I made myself focus on the cords that ran along the floor, from the people's elbows and out of the pool, across the room, where they were hooked into a wall of computers, just like the robot had been. Just like I'd drawn.

"It's all the original test group," I whispered. "From the newspaper article."

"Oh, no," Rose said. "This is Bio-Rite II and III. You were Bio-Rite IV."

"Where's Bio-Rite I?"

Rose shook her head with mock sadness. "Zero percent viability. Poor quality test-stock. Your local transients and runaways, mostly. That's what happens when you cut corners and go with lower-grade material."

A guy in the corner of the pool started to jerk, like a dog in the middle of a dream.

"They're having afterlives, aren't they?"

"Exactly," Rose said proudly. "They're busy being rock stars and billionaires and athletes and stewardess-gropers."

It was tempting to hand over the comic and lie on the floor and have the nervous breakdown that'd been knocking on my door for a year.

"So Mr. Puglisi lied. There's no vacuum store, no one died. They've all been here all along."

"He didn't *lie*." Rose laughed. "He's software. He did what he was programmed to do."

I thought about all the kids at school. Zac, Dayna, the six dozen Kirstys. I thought about the clothes they wore, the cars they drove, who they picked on, who they were nice to.

"Don't we all just do what we're programmed to do?"

"That's very deep, Ayn Rand," Rose said. "But the answer is no. We're all in control of our own decisions. Free will is the only will. Like, for instance, how I freely decided to get rich. And how I'm about to."

I pointed to the people in the pool. "They're not in control of their decisions."

"They made a choice," Rose said. "They volunteered."

"For this?"

"For a fantasy. Which is exactly what they got. Of course, they probably didn't read the fine print. Five minutes of being a rock star, and then the real show starts. You want some advice? Always read the fine print."

"What real show?"

"The assembly-line show. They're dreaming of factory workers. Building product. High-end televisions, designer shoes. Laptops. Scooters. Maybe in year two we can move to food. Steaks, lobster, Chilean sea bass."

"Why? What good does it do you?"

"None at all," Rose said. "Until someone with perseverance, smarts, and loads of business acumen figured out a way to reopen the Conduit."

"God, do you suck," I said.

"Don't act so superior. After all, if your father had sold the program to, say, the Chinese military, who knows what they'd be bringing out? Ray guns? An army of minotaurs? Mao's long-lost brother Fred Tse-tung?"

"So why tell me?" I asked. "Why don't you just shoot me and get it over with."

"Oh, I would never shoot you, honeypot," Rose said. "The code we injected in you has finally gestated, which happens to take —"

"— exactly one year?"

"Have I said happy birthday yet?"

"Yes."

"You're special, Sophie." Rose sighed, putting her hand on my shoulder. "You're the only test subject to ever succeed. You're like Amelia Earhart. Or Wilma Rudolf. You've gone where no one else ever has. Your potential is limitless."

I tried not to blush. It was mortifying, but even coming from her, I liked it. It felt good to be touched. I hated myself for being so weak.

"The code inside you is a Trojan horse," Rose said. "Once you jack in directly, it'll force the Conduit open. This time we'll keep it open. It'll be like we're partners."

"What about my father?" I whispered, forcing myself to push her hand away.

Rose shuffled to a desk in the corner. In the center was a tiny white hard drive. It hummed loudly, pulsing with little waves of light. There were no wires coming from it except a single orange extension cord that ran along the floor, snaking all the way to the far wall, where it was plugged in to a transformer.

"After his theft was discovered, I gave Albert a few choices. Having a private talk in a windswept field with our Russian investors was one. Volunteering to be a petrie dish was another. Your father is . . . permanently connected."

I started to back away. Her eyes were suddenly huge and black.

"But don't worry, sweetie, *Popsicle Man 3.0* has a very important purpose. Your father and his little truck haul goods from the Conduit to the physical warehouse."

I turned to run, but Rose's arm lashed out like a buzzard's claw and grabbed me by the wrist, just as she'd done a year ago.

"Hey!"

Rose dug her long nails into my arm, chunking beneath the surface. She yanked, tearing the skin at my elbow backward. I screamed but couldn't wrestle away. She tore in even farther, ripping up a flap the size of a tennis ball. My legs wavered. Nausea rushed through me. Blood leaked from the jagged wound, but not as much as there should have been.

"That's your hookup," Rose said, letting go. "It's been growing all year. Now it's fully formed." She held out a gold-tipped stereo plug attached to a thick rubber cord, which coiled from the hard drive. "Jack on in and you can ask your father all about it."

I stared at my arm. Below the torn flap of skin, between bone and ligament and vein, was a fleshy cylindrical tube, like the tip of a hollow straw. It quivered pinkly as if it were anticipating accepting the plug. Rose held her cord. In the crook of her arm was a withered nub. "C'mon, we'll jack in together."

I took the cord, turning it over in my hand. I wanted to fling it like a snake, but part of me wanted to hold it even more. My jack continued to quiver, like someone was twanging a string, a thrumming bass-line. It was sensitive and itchy and raw. It also felt relieved, as if it were finally allowed to breathe.

"You feel it, I know you do," Rose said.

The jack began to ache, desperate for the plug to enter it. For the circle to be complete. For the numbers to come into me, ones and zeros, but not in dreams anymore.

"Plug it in," Rose whispered huskily. "It'll make the injection seem like a baby toy. This is pure feed. Top of the line."

I could almost hear the numbers daring me with tiny laughing whispers. *Do it do it do it do it.*

"Plug it in," Rose said again, already connected. Her face went slack as it took effect. "It feels like a thousand exploding suns."

I held the plug an inch from the opening. My hand shook. There was still time to run. She couldn't stop me. I could take the drawings and go back out to the car and drive to . . . to . . .

"Your brother is going to be Bio-Rite V, you know," Rose slurred. "You're paving the way for the next generation."

Kenny. I had to go find him. But I was suddenly utterly exhausted, resistance bleeding away with each pulse of my elbow. I wanted that jack inside me. I wanted to know the rest of what was going on. Everything. No more lies.

Do it do it do it do it.

Find Kenny. Stop this. Resist.

Do it do it do it do it.

Run. Upstairs. Now.

Do it do it do it do it.

I handed Rose *The Adventures of Destruktor-Bot and Manny Solo, Boy Mentor.* She cradled it, a smile on her face like the Grinch teetering above Whoville.

"Screw it," I said, completely letting go.

"That's right," Rose hissed. "Screw it in. Righty-tighty."

I clenched my teeth and shoved the plug, savagely, jamming it as deep and as hard as it would go.

CHAPTER SEVEN
NIGHT RIDERS AND
TOE CUTTERS

SORT OF LIKE TRON, BUT WITH BETTER EFFECTS

The Popsicle truck tore down the highway. It was a beautiful day, the sky luminously blue through big panel windows in front while the sun shone in from the sides and rear. I was in the hold. Next to me on the bench seats were Dayna Daynes, Coach Dhushbak, Aaron, Miss Last, Bryce Ballar, and half a dozen squealy blond Kirstys. It was the test group from the newspaper article.

"Now we're talking," Bryce said, slapping me five. "I knew you could do it!"

"Do what?"

"It was a test, Gothika. You totally passed!"

"Whooo!" said the Kirstys, doing an impromptu cheer.

"We've all been through it," he said. "At some point, you gotta decide if you're gonna plug in, and you did!" Bryce rubbed his neck, whistling in a low, impressed tone. "I took days just staring at the white cube before I got up the nerve to jack that shit. Bam, right in the arm, huh? Crazy. But you? You know how long you were standing there, trying to decide?"

"Forever," Kirsty Templeton laughed.

"Forever," Dayna Daynes agreed.

"But now you're here," Bryce said. "We're all together again."

The truck took a long, swerving left, and everyone leaned into it. There was a feeling of jollity and freedom and excitement. There was a sense of incredible relief. Was it true? Had I actually done something good? They all started talking at once, like in a locker room, taking turns going on about the dreams they had, the people they'd been.

"I ran this crappy karaoke place in Seoul! If I ever hear 'Sister Ray' again, I swear I am seriously gonna slit wrist!"

"I was a chemist in a dog-food factory. All day long I'm like, what do I add to this pile of sawdust to make it taste more like home-cooked gravy?"

"I was a car salesman. I'm standing there shaking hands, like, hey, you want to put twenty percent down on a new Mercedes StatusSled LE, or should we go old-school and lease a Hummer with the full Esteem Monster package?"

I laughed and stood up, hanging on to one of the freezers as the truck took another corner. They all seemed so happy. Had we really been going through this together all along?

"I knew you could do it," Bryce said again.

The Kirstys got all excited and started randomly hugging each other, so the guys got up and shook hands and slapped backs.

"Best student I ever had," Coach Dhushbak said, giving me a wink. "I'm canceling all your detentions for the rest of the year!"

Dayna Daynes stepped over, looking ashamed. "Listen, about the way I've acted . . . I didn't know why I —"

"Don't worry about it," I said.

Behind Dayna, Aaron was waiting his turn. "You and me?" He smiled. "When there's not so many people around? We need to spend some serious time. You feelin' me, boo?"

I nodded, turning toward the front. A man in a white lab coat was behind the wheel. He adjusted the rearview mirror and blew me a kiss.

"Dad?"

My father pulled the truck off the highway and down an exit ramp, into a cul-de-sac with big yards and nice houses and swing sets. He turned the organ grinder music as loud as it would go, and dozens of children came running after us. Bryce and Coach

Dhushbak and the others filed out of the truck and started handing out free ice creams. My father squeezed my hand, in no hurry, opening the freezers and letting anyone take whatever they wanted. The kids cheered. They tore off wrappers and chased one another in circles. They kicked balls and shared Fudgesicles and dripped all over their shirts.

My father finally turned and stood in front of me. He looked the same, young and serious, with his thick glasses and wavy hair. He took me in his arms and buried his face in my neck. I squeezed him back. We stood that way a long time, until he gently let me go. He kissed me on the forehead and then took my hand, leading me toward a lush field of grass. The sun was beaming. I slipped off my shoes. The grass felt amazing on my toes. All around us were picnic tables and sandboxes and swing sets. Off in a stand of pines was a marble pool surrounded by statuary. We walked toward it. A stone cherub stood on one foot in the center, spitting in a glistening arc. The water looked clean and clear and deep.

"I knew this day would come," he said as we sat together, a little smile on his face. "I just had to wait a year. Until we were both ready. Even so, I can hardly believe you're here."

I looked at my lap. He took my hand and squeezed it. "It's okay, Soph. I know there's been so much confusion, so much to doubt. It's what she did to all of us. But I'm so proud of you. You hung in there. The first test group? Well, let's just say most of them spend a lot of time sniffing their fingertips and talking to walls. And the second group didn't fare much better. But you know what? In the end, all our sacrifices will be worth it. Each and every one of us will be treated like heroes. Your friends, the coach, the freckled boy. There will be magazines, talk shows. You want to be on Bloprah? Chatterman? This project is going to change the world. When the Conduit opens, just think what we can bring out! The possibilities are limitless!"

The thing is, I *had* been thinking about it. And it scared me to death. Limitless possibility actually seemed like a curse. If you could bring out anything good, you could bring out anything bad. If everyone could be cured of disease, we'd all live to a hundred and fifty and there'd be no room for anyone to live. If we were all suddenly rich, pretty soon there'd be no reason to do anything at all. Whatever you wanted would just come out of the tube. Cars or houses or yachts. We'd all become content and fat. And then they'd bring out a pill to make us skinny. Or a pill to make us think being fat was better, after all. And eventually, people would find a way to fight over the Conduit. Someone would decide they had to be in control, even if you brought out a pill that made no one want to be in control. Once the conveyor belts got rolling, there would have to be trucks and planes and ships to move the stuff around the world. India needs rice. Germany needs leather pants. Australia needs shrimp skewers. And then they'd have to bring out the gas to fuel the planes. And then the pilots to fly them. And then the machines to train the robot pilots, since no one wanted to work anymore. It would all just keep happening over and over again, a solution for every solution, until the whole world was so full of discarded junk there would be nowhere to sit.

My father was smiling at me, waiting for my response. I could tell he thought I was dreaming of all the things I could have, the new stereos and watches and clothes. I looked away. Near us, a family was picnicking. Two squirrels in a tree shared a shiny acorn. A pair of robins cooed and billed against each other. Maybe I was being too cynical. Maybe there was a way that everything could be figured out. Rules could be decided on, and the whole thing could be made fair. Maybe there was a way for the whole world to be as beautiful and still and warm as it was here, in the grass, right now.

Yeah, maybe.

"Do you see now, honey?" My father said. "Do you see why we had to go through what we did? Why it will all be worth it?"

I didn't see. I wanted to ask him about the things Rose had

shown me. I wanted to ask him about being run over by the truck, and his leaving Trish, and his lying to me. I opened my mouth, but his expression was so open and trusting, I couldn't do it. It was so nice just to be with him again, sitting in the sun, holding hands. The questions could wait a minute.

"Dad?"

"Yes, honey?"

"I have something I have to admit."

"Mmm-hmm."

"After you left, in a way I was almost glad you were gone."

My father stared at me.

"I realize now, your leaving sort of justified my being miserable. I started to think if things were going to go bad, they might as well go *really* bad, you know? Like I was Joan of Arc or something."

"There is no percentage in mediocre suffering," he said. "You might as well corner the market."

"Exactly," I smiled, relieved he understood. "Your being gone was such a good excuse, I knew I could be a total screwup, and deep down, no one could blame me."

My father nodded and held up a pink ice-cream cone. "Hey, have you tried this flavor? It's delicious."

I shook my head. "I don't want any —"

Grrrr . . . erf erf erf!

Twinkle came tearing across the lawn and jumped onto my lap, licking my face. Her little body trembled with happiness.

"But wait . . . how?" I laughed as she bowled me over. We rolled on the grass and I pressed her tightly against my chest, tracing the circle on her belly with my finger.

"Is that good?" my father asked. "Does that work?"

Twinkle chewed my knuckle. "Work?"

He shrugged. His smile was unwavering.

I looked down at my dog. The color of her hair was a tiny bit different than I remembered. "But I saw her out there. In the vat."

"Your trust made this all possible, honey," my father said.

"That doesn't mean anything."

"Having the courage to work through the confusion," he said. "Being strong and confident. A new you, a silver lining."

I knew my dog was dead. I pushed this Twinkle away, but she thought I was playing a game and jumped on me again. I grabbed her with two hands and tossed her farther. Twinkle let out a yip, and then a little growl. Her big anime eyes looked sad, but I could also see a glint of resentment. She raised a lip and slunk away.

"Don't be a party pooper, Soph," my father said. "Let's keep it real. You and me just kickin' it."

"Stop speaking in clichés!" I said.

He looked down at his hands and wiped at the corner of his eye, where a tear dutifully began to fall.

"I want to know where Kenny is," I said.

"He'll be here soon, don't worry."

"But I *am* worried. I'm starting to —"

My father slapped his hands together. "But enough talking about old times, Soph! Let's roll up our sleeves and get to work! Let's open up that Conduit!" His eyes narrowed excitedly. "When we do, there won't be a Nobel big enough! There won't be enough grants and awards for them to give us!"

"What about those people back there?" I said. "In the pool. Those *volunteers*. When do they get their awards?"

"Innovation requires sacrifice," he said.

I let go of his hand. "It's not a sacrifice when people don't know they're giving something up. I didn't know. O.S. didn't know. Were you ready to sacrifice us, too?"

My father rubbed beneath his glasses. "You're not listening."

"And what about the senior class? I saw the paperwork. The school lied to them. The lab tricked them. You've injected them all."

"No! That was her idea," he said disgustedly. "Prepping them as the next test group? I was completely against it."

"Yeah, and what about her?" I said. "You and her?"

He stood up, trying to get a grip on himself. He was all facade. I could see right through him. He was a little boy who wanted to sit in a corner and play with his gadgets and be told how smart he was.

"You did something to me," I said. "Didn't you?"

He wrapped his arms around his chest and twirled in a circle three times, like he was trying to make himself dizzy.

"Answer me," I said.

He put his hands over his ears. "I'm never getting out, am I?" he asked, in a singsong voice, over and over, "never, never, never."

In the distance, the sun had started to go down. The Popsicle truck turned dark, as if it had begun to rust.

"What's happening?"

My father began to shake. The beautiful green grass below us turned brown. Bryce and Aaron disappeared. The laughing children disappeared. The clouds turned black and the birds began to peck at one other. The squirrels bared their fangs. I could see the Kirstys, across the street in someone's lawn, joined at the hip like Siamese twins. They had four heads but one torso, just one pair of legs, which ran in circles while they screamed and pulled each other's hair.

"The Rumor," I whispered, but my father was gone. It was suddenly sweaty hot. Everything began to drip thickly, humid and pungent. There was a thrum in the background. It started in my feet and worked up my calves. It itched and ached in turn, clawing. I slapped and rubbed at myself, but it continued along my sides, like marching bees, stinging at random.

"Stop!"

I ran toward the pool as my father's desperation came at me in waves, like cheap cologne. It permeated everything, a high wire of pain arcing from him into me. It was everything, the grass and the dirt and the sky. It seeped into my pores, under my fingernails. It smelled like bad mayonnaise, like hundreds of pig's tails, like a thousand Sour Whites. His thoughts fell in sheets, numbers raining down in whispered apologies and admissions.

"Stop!"

I could hear his voice in my head. *Switch places.*

It was tiny and scared. *Sophie, switch places with me.*

The sky and the grass began to whirl. I knew the answer to the questions I hadn't had a chance to ask. It was all about survival. It was all about preservation. He'd run me over again and again, trying to get me to come here. He wanted me to give the comic to The Nurse. He wanted me to jack in. He wanted me to take his place.

Switch switch switch switch.

I looked down into the pool. The cherub had cracked and fallen on its side. The water was boiling, tuning pink. Trees were falling all around me. The ground began to open in huge, shearing cracks.

I stood on the lip and dove in.

CHAPTER SIX
KENNY BLUE BLAND

DON'T MESS WITH THE SPICE

Oh, man, is Lake okay?"

Herb waved off my question. "What do you say, young Mr. Spice, that you start by telling me everything you know about all this weirdness Lake was mentioning earlier?"

"Sure," I said. His stare was making me nervous. I sat up, making space on the floor for my feet, kicking blenders and tennis balls and melon scoops and visors and electronics manuals and cookie sheets under the couch. I told him about Sophie's not sleeping. About her dreams. About her fear of ice cream. About The Nurse. It sounded completely dumb, but Herb nodded along.

"Then, there's my father and everything. Being gone and so forth? Without any explanation? I'd say that's the lodestone of weird in our family. Also, there's the comic."

"The comic," Herb said, licking his lips, not a question. "You brought it with you."

I reached in my bag, which was soaked through with sweat. *Destruktor-Bot* wasn't there. I pulled out *Leatherface and Rayon-foot #42*, which was wet to the binding, a Fair-minus or worse. *Fumble Carrot #13* was in even rougher shape. The cover disintegrated in my hand. I checked in the bag again. No Bot. No Manny Solo. I dumped it all out onto the couch. There were wrappers and peels and crumpled foil. It was the first time in an entire year I didn't have Dad's comic with me.

"Um? I guess it's not here."

"Predictable," Herb said, his jaw clenched. "It's all starting to come together."

"What is?"

"Randomness. Chaos. Random and chaotic weirdness. It comes in cycles."

"How so?"

"Well," Herb said, leaning back, "me knowing your father and all, for one."

"You *knew* him?"

"I used to be a guard there, over at ol' Fade Labs. Actually, I heard tell of you, too. Just some whispers in the hallway. Come to think of it, I don't know that O.S. stands for Overwhelmingly Studious at all." Herb grinned. "Little bit lying to me there, huh, Kenneth? Actually, I think O.S. stands for Organic Sample."

"Kenneth," Lake mumbled, "is short for Kenny."

"That's a really strange coincidence," I said. "That you —"

"It's not a coincidence at all," Herb said, tapping the knife he'd cut my blanket-shirt with on his thigh. *Tap tap tap. Tappity tap tap.* "Everyone in this town has worked for the lab at one time or another. One way or another. We're all sort of a big family. Money for the school, money for the library. Money for personal subsidies, hush money, bail, lawsuits. Really, my point is, everyone's connected, all of us. It is both a philosophy and a reality. Win or lose."

"Um, win what?"

Herb smiled. His mustache twitched.

The phone rang. Lake wheeled over and picked it up. "Yeah, he's sitting right here," she said. "Wearing a blanket." She replaced the receiver.

"Tell me about my father," I whispered.

Lake lit two cigarettes at the same time, giving one to Herb. His had lipstick on the filter. Herb took a deep drag, letting the smoke slowly curl from his nose, smudges of red on his bottom lip.

"Your father was something of an artist himself. Liked to draw pictures and show them to us lowly guards on his lunch break. Maybe give us a little lecture about science. Be the big man, knowing all he knew. Being all he was, and us being all we weren't. He got some people fired, you know. Being a stickler. Rules this, rules that. Yeah, me and the guys, we got a real kick out of your old man's pictures."

I started to take the blanket off. "Maybe I should go."

"You're not going anywhere, Mr. Organic," Herb said, while Lake slowly rolled between me and the door.

Herb strapped Lake into the van and secured her chair. He strapped me in behind her, his fingers on the back of my neck, digging in.

"You don't need to do that," I said.

"You have no idea what I need." He grinned, winding the extra tethers around my wrists and ankles. He slung the doors closed and walked around front. Soon, the van tore down the highway.

"So, how do you figure ol' Gothika's doing right about now?" Herb asked, half turning in his seat.

"Excuse me?"

"Hey, Mr. Organic," he said polishing his front teeth with the tie he'd put on. "Did you know that the Goths were actually a tribe that invaded Rome around A.D. five hundred?"

"I may have, you know, read that somewhere?" I said, not bothering to mention I'd read it in *Vandals vs. Danes vs. Huns #12, The Berserker Wars.*

Herb frowned. "Did you know that A.D. does not stand for After Death?"

I poked Lake's arm, but she just stared out the window.

"It stands for anno Domini," I said.

"Correct," Herb said. "And what does anno Domini mean?"

"Year of the Donut?"

"Smart guy," Herb said. "Just like your father."

"Not really," I said.

The van careened across three lanes of traffic, down a curling exit ramp, across an intersection, and along the waterfront. Herb shifted into low, punching it over a set of railroad tracks, and pulled sideways into the parking lot of White, Fade, Templeton, and Sour.

"Honey, we're home!" he said.

"What are we doing?"

"Time to jack in."

"Time to what?"

Herb shook his head sadly. "You could fill a computer with everything you don't know." He unstrapped Lake, lowered her chair on the lift, then waved, slamming the door shut.

"Um, hello? Wait?"

Herb opened the lab door without looking back, wheeling Lake in. I pulled at the tethers that held my legs, which only made them tighter and hurt more. I stared around the van. There were at least three hundred random things strewn around, none of them looking particularly sharp. So I banged my head against the wheel-well for a while. It was hollow and made a nice thumping sound. Did it hurt? Yeah, sorta.

I considered my options: None.

What would Manny Solo, boy mentor, do?

CHAPTER FIVE
SOPHIE BLUE

I'D LAUGH IF SOMEONE HAD BOTHERED
TO PROGRAM ME A MOUTH

I was back in the white lab, dripping wet. It was empty except for the equipment.

"Hello?"

The hard drive still sat on the table, humming. I tried to lift it so I could smash it on the floor, but it wouldn't budge.

Pull the cord.

I reached for the extension that linked the hard drive to a bank of computers against the wall. As I did, the people in the pool began to make noise, a low, steady moan. They all seemed to hit the same note, which got progressively louder and more forlorn. I didn't want to hurt them, but I couldn't let this place, this program, or my father exist for even one more second. I curled another loop of the extension around my fist. The moaning from the pool exploded, a wanton throb that echoed off the walls.

"Hold on there, partner," a young Rose Fade said, skipping over to her desk. She was coltish, beautiful, vibrant. She casually picked up the other end of the cord. "How's it feel to be plugged straight in?"

I looked down at my elbow. There was nothing there, but I could feel it, pulsing. "I'm thirsty," I said. "And hungry."

"Not surprising," Rose said. "You've been standing there for hours."

"Hours?"

"Acclimating. Playing footsie with your father. It takes a while for the euphoria to wear off."

I remembered the enormous rush when the jack first went in, my back arching, the explosion of code entering me. There were starbursts, amoebic slides, long multicolored trails. I didn't want to admit that I'd enjoyed it so much.

"It gets better every time," Rose whispered, gently pulling up the cord's slack. I stepped toward the hard drive as the plug began to inch from the computer.

"Okay, okay!" she said, giving up ground. It was gratifying to see her nervous. She'd said I was special before. Maybe it wasn't a bunch of shit. Maybe in here I really could do things other people couldn't. Bring back physical items. Resist my lunatic father. If I could turn the Conduit on, maybe I could turn things off, too.

Pull the cord.

Rose pointed behind me. It was too stupid to be a trick. "Someone's here to see you."

A tall blond girl walked from the back of the warehouse, sashaying like a model. She was wearing an expensive dress and high heels. She stood next to Rose. They held hands.

"Hi."

The girl's eyes were amazingly green. She was tall, almost regal in her posture. She smiled at me without an ounce of friendliness.

"Lake?" I said. "But —"

"I can walk in here, that's why, genius."

I blinked and rubbed my eyes. "How long have you . . . ?"

"Since all along." Lake pulled up her sleeve, showing me her jack. "Like, you're so special?"

I couldn't swallow. It was too much.

"This whole time? This whole time you . . . ?"

"Boo-hoo," Lake said.

"Whiner," Rose said, and they giggled, leaning over and whispering to each other. It was like being in the caf. Me, at my own table, as usual.

"But why?" I said. It was too depressing to ask, but I had to know.

Lake swung her long hair around, combing it with two fingers. "Why else? So I can be like I was."

"How's that supposed to happen?"

"Some experiment," Lake said. "They're injecting something in my spine. Bio-Rite or whatever."

"But Bio-Rite doesn't work."

Lake pulled lipstick from her waist pocket and put on a new coat. Then she lit an unfiltered cigarette, clenching it in her teeth. "Okay, so I'll stay in here."

"Stay?"

Lake did a back handspring. She did three cartwheels and then the splits, raising two imaginary pom-poms and giving them a spirit-filled shake. "Whoo, Go Toros!"

"It's not real."

"You?" she laughed. "*You're* the person who decides what's real?"

"But you said —"

"I said what I had to say!" she almost yelled. "What, like I'm just going to accept it? I didn't *fall*. They dropped me! So I get to spend the rest of my life doing physical therapy? The monkey bars and gymnastics mats and saying I just can't do it, until I find the Eye of the Tiger and heal myself through positivity and pure will? Screw that. Especially when Chad and Tinky offered to pay for a shortcut."

"What shortcut?"

"The clinic, moron. They're all, like, but 'Part of the deal is you have to go babysit this mopey depressive.' I swear, I'd rather have had Daddy pay another hundred grand."

"They *sent* you to my house?"

Lake laughed. "Do you think I would hang out with you on purpose?"

I wasn't going to cry. I was definitely *not* going to cry.

"Honeypot!" Herb said, walking in from the back of the room. I was about to run over and throw my arms around his neck and beg him to carry me out of here. Then he sat at Rose's desk, put his feet up, and started cleaning his nails with a letter opener.

"You, too? Really, Herb?"

"Well, you know what they say," Lake said. "Sometimes paranoia is just having all the facts."

Rose slapped her five.

I coiled the cord, about to yank it, hard. Rose yanked back. Lake rushed over and grabbed Rose's end. I leaned as far away from them as I could, grunting. The cord began to cut into my hands. My arm was going numb. They pulled and swore, beads of sweat rolling down their foreheads, but they were losing. I was stronger. I was actually stronger.

The plug began to quiver at the outlet. One prong got loose.

"Don't!" Rose said.

"Don't!" Lake said.

Another prong came loose.

"Kenny will be deleted, too!" Rose hissed, letting go. The cord went slack and I fell back against the wall, slamming my head and sliding down onto my butt. Lake came over and knelt next to me. "She's right, you know. So go ahead and pull. One less lard-ass in the world, what difference does it make?"

Herb grinned. "Hey, now, what if it's a trick? What if unplugging it is what she really *wants* you to do? Maybe you're going to make everything worse! Oh, boy, what a dilemma!"

I closed my eyes. They were playing games with me because they knew I had the power to stop them. It wasn't a trick. I really was special. They'd been maneuvering me for a year, getting me to this spot for a reason. For everything good you could bring out, there would be something just as bad. And I was it. I *was* the bad thing. For her.

"On the other hand," Herb said, "there's the question of your brother, and how this may affect him. Or even kill him. Decisions, decisions."

I could almost sense that Kenny was close. The jack in my elbow twitched like a dowser, as if it could feel him, too. And if he was close, whatever happened to me would probably happen to him as well. We were linked, just as we always had been. If Kenny was going to be deleted, then so would I. At least we'd do it together. Actually, it would probably be the best thing that ever happened to either of us.

"I saw a poster once," Herb said. "It was a picture of a darkhaired girl standing in front of two identical doors. One had a comedy mask painted on it. The other had a tragedy mask. Underneath it said *Go Ahead and Pick, Loser Chick*."

The moaning got louder. The people in the pool were kicking their legs in tandem. The water began to froth.

"Don't do it," Rose said. "Think of your father."

I tightened my grip.

"Your brother," Lake said. "Think of your brother."

I was thinking of my brother. Always. So I pulled.

00101001010101010010101010101000010101111010110.

There was a blink. Everything went black and then white, and then faded to blue.

CHAPTER FOUR
KENNY BLUE

ARE YOU TALKING TO ME? ARE YOU TALKING TO *ME?*

H oo, boy, do my wrists ache? You bet. They're actually tore up pretty good. I look like I tried to kill myself with a butter knife. Twice. But it's nothing compared to my gums. I mean, it took *forever* to bite my way out of the tethers. They tasted a little like grilled chicken. At least that's what I tried to tell myself, swallowing strand after strand of oily yellow plastic.

The front door was open, and the second door, too.

"Hello?"

The lab seemed deserted. My voice echoed among the trash and glass and broken computers. I poked around for a while, as quietly as I could, not wanting to run into Herb. Pretty much ever again.

"Lake?" I whispered, but there was no answer.

On the floor was a long piece of lead pipe. I picked it up, hefting it. With the proper angle and torque, would it split skull? Definitely. I walked from office to office, slapping it in my palm, feeling a mix of tough-cool and utterly ridiculous.

"Sophie?"

There was nothing. No elevator, no stairs, no scientists, no Herb, no Lake. Just a bunch of broken junk and wet carpet and wires strung from wall to wall. I sat down on a rusty desk and considered my options: none. My elbow itched, like the worst poison ivy. My nails needed to be trimmed. I scratched away anyhow, really letting them dig in. The pipe fell onto the carpet with a dull noise, rolling away from me. It rolled to the far wall and then disappeared into the shadows in the corner, clanging down what sounded like metal steps. A lot of metal steps.

CHAPTER THREE
SOPHIE, LAKE, TRISH, KENNY, HERB

AND MICHAEL AND JANET AND LATOYA AND JERMAINE

Sophie Blue yawned and stretched. Miss Last had chalk on her face and collar and shirt, like she usually did. Sophie realized she'd been asked a question and the class was waiting. There was a long silence.

"Null set?"

"Correct," Miss Last said, turning back to the board and outlining another problem. Eventually the bell rang, and everyone streamed out into the hallway. In front of the girls' bathroom, Bryce Ballar was hassling some freshman. Sophie caught his eye, and he nodded blandly, without recognition. In the mirror in the girls' bathroom, Sophie stared at her own face. Clean and clear. She wasn't a boy. She was definitely not the star of the basketball team. She was just herself, unremarkable. Gothika.

"You can stop looking at yourself," said Dayna Daynes as she kicked open a stall with her high heel. "There's not much to see."

"I know, isn't it great?"

Dayna snorted. "Um, that was an insult?"

Sophie turned and looked at Dayna in the mirror. "You have a birthmark on your hip. Shaped like a half-moon. And you do this dumb backward swirl with your tongue when you French kiss, and you make funny squirrel noises when you're excited. And you're a really, really, really boring date."

Dayna Daynes's jaw hung open, but she said nothing. A fly

circled and landed on her lip. Sophie walked into the hall, drying her hands on her tiny black skirt.

Screaming kids pushed and shoved their way onto the bus. All of them had handheld games and Walkmans and Eye-pods and headphones and new jackets and new jeans and shiny sneakers. Some of them were wearing multiple headphones. Some of the kids threw their stuff at each other and out the window. Brand-new cell phones and mini hard drives were smashed along the roadway. Sophie had her own seat, as usual, alone. There was a long, loud, annoying ride across town. It was beautiful. Who owned a Jeep? Or a red convertible? No one. The bus drove slowly and carefully, past strip mall after strip mall, the stores over-flowing with products. Each one was having a *huge sale,* or *item blowout,* or *price slash frenzy.* All the houses seemed to have two or three cars in the driveway. There were old televisions in every garbage can, toys on the lawns, shiny new bikes and skateboards and scooters collecting in piles everywhere. There were un-opened boxes in garages and long slings of wrapping paper and plastic that wafted across the streets like tumbleweeds.

At home, Trish was in the kitchen, making dinner in a new dress. Her hair was combed and she was wearing makeup. She actually looked pretty. Herb McLean sat at the table reading the *Wall Street Journal.* He was in a three-piece suit and had a fresh martini on the table in front of him. His legs were crossed, show-ing argyle socks.

"Soph!" he said. "How was school?"

"Great!" Sophie said, and slapped him five. Trish laughed and then squeezed Herb's shoulder. Next to him were a bunch of un-opened printer boxes. There were also stacks of gameboyz, cal-culators, and ink cartridges.

"You want to buy one?" Herb said. "I got all the models."

"No, thanks," Sophie said.

Herb pulled mp3 players from his pocket. "You want one of these? They got music. They got games. I got more in the basement if you —"

"I'm broke," Sophie said, and went down to Kenny's room, where he was listening to music and lifting weights. Lake sat next to him, giving him tips on form and reps.

Kenny winked at Sophie, while Lake corrected his form. "You're doing great!"

Kenny put the barbell back on its supports. One of her CDs, Lightly Seasoned Orphans, blared out of his little radio, "Oh don't stay under," the singer warbled, "don't stay under too too long. . . ."

"What're you doing, O.S.?" Sophie asked.

"Kenneth's trying out for the team," Lake said, wheeling away from the door.

"Kenneth?"

"Football," Kenny said. "I think maybe I have the size for it. It's going to be pretty great."

Lake smiled. She picked up a magazine and started leafing through the pages. Sophie realized Lake was wearing a dress as well, a lot like Trish's. She also had on makeup and had shaved her legs. Behind her, on the wall, was a poster. It was a picture of a cow standing on two legs in the middle of a muddy field. Underneath it said *It's All So Udderly Perfect*.

"Hey," Sophie asked, "you guys want to come upstairs and hang out?"

Kenny raised one eyebrow. Sophie blinked, and it seemed for a second like her brother had mouthed something to her, turning away from Lake. *Take my hand.* Sophie blinked, and then it was gone. He was smiling again.

"Um, I can't?" Kenny said with a big grin. "I have some great stuff to do."

"Stuff?" Sophie said.

"We have stuff," Lake said, wheeling back over. "To do."

Sophie looked around Kenny's basement room. It was nice and clean now, with new shades, even though there was no window, and a new light fixture that hung from the ceiling. There were stacks of unopened video games and components and computer parts still in boxes. There were shrink-wrapped shoes and wires and pin-striped suits. She could hear Trish talking to the TV upstairs and her quiet laugh. It was an overwhelming sensation, Sophie thought, knowing she was just a girl. Small and untalented and without special powers or knowledge. Maybe it was time to get a job. Like, at one of the new stores. The thought filled her with satisfaction.

"I think I really like things this way, you know?" she finally said. "All of us one big family? Everything just seems really great now."

"I hope so." Kenny grinned. He made a muscle for her. "How else could it be?"

Sophie went into the hallway and dialed Information. Then she dialed the number the computer gave her. A woman answered.

"Hello? Is Aaron there?"

After a while a voice came on the line. "Hello?"

"Hi. This is Sophie Blue."

"Um . . . yeah?"

"Hey, Aaron, you want to go to the prom with me?"

There was a long pause. Finally, Aaron cleared his throat. "No."

It was Sophie's turn to clear her throat. "Okay. Sorry if I bothered you."

"You know what I hate?" Aaron said. "People who apologize all the time. Also, I hate getting dressed. In some dumb rental tuxedo. How about we just buy some sodas. And climb the hillside above town. And drink them lying in the grass. While we make out."

Sophie laughed. "Great!"

"Great," he said. "I'll see you. In an hour."

Sophie went upstairs and looked in her mom's closet for just the right dress, trying a few on. Maybe she'd been acting out all along, you know? I mean, who wore Catholic skirts? And by the way, wasn't that an excellent name for a band. Catho*LICK*skirt? Like, with umlauts over the *K*? No, actually it wasn't. It was a really dumb idea. Where did that thought come from? There was definitely no reason to write it down or draw it. And, to tell you the truth, maybe it was time to wipe off all the eyeliner. Sophie looked at herself in the mirror, a pink dress draped in front of her, turning this way and that. It was nice, the way the material felt. It was pretty. And soft, like how you could touch it, and the way it felt in your hand. Sophie unzipped the back and put it on. Perfect. It was totally weird, but she was suddenly positive that from here on out, everything was going to be really, really great. Maybe this weekend she could get the whole gang together for a super-fun trip to the pool.

CHAPTER TWO
LA NUTRIKA

THE PRICE OF PURE EVIL. WELL, MAYBE NOT PURE, BUT DEFINITELY PRETTY SOLIDLY EVILISH

Yeah, yeah, Nutrika is Latin or something for *nurse*. Buy yourself a dictionary, cheapskate. Hey, you know what's funny? People will buy anything if you position it right. Like a whole company, or a software program, or even the illusion that they are safe and sound. The illusion of normality. Let me tell you something, if things seem normal in this world, something has gone to vinegar. Something's off. My advice? Don't buy it. For even a second. Hey, but that's just me.

Do you have any idea how hard it was to rise in the corporate world as an intelligent, capable woman? I didn't think so. Well, it's not just hard, it's nearly impossible. But I did it. By being tougher. And smarter. And mostly just telling people what they wanted to hear. "Oh, I love you, I burn for you, I need your touch." You know, something like that, but sprinkle in a little of the sincere. Or, you're like, "Everything is okay now, just turn off this switch and you can go home." You know, dangle a carrot. People believe what they want to believe. You just need to give them the room to convince themselves.

Yeah, so Dynatone/Glazo finally got over their "ethical" concerns, which really just means they found some expert who needed to settle his gambling debts, and decided to acquire the Virtuality. All of it. *PopsicleMan 3.0, The Conduit 2.0, Assembly-Line 1.0.* Hey, here's the keys, so enjoy! Whatever happens now, happens. I'm an old woman, even if I don't look it, and what old woman doesn't need round-the-clock attention from a tanned manservant? Well, this one does. And that kind of thing costs some serious green. Just the kind of green I now have in my off-shore account. Accounts. Anyway, my theory is, everything happens for a reason, and people end up where they belong. Like, for instance, in a virtual slum-factory screwing together Eye-Pods and Dikes on twenty-four-hour shifts. And, conversely, I belong here, on my travertine patio, with the Mediterranean gently lapping the foundation of my centuries-old villa, a nice wine and cheese plate laid before me. A woman has to do what a woman has to do to get by in this world. Have I mentioned that yet? And if some multinational bloodsucker of a company wants to re-ward that woman with millions of dollars in stock options, well, that's their business, isn't it? And if that company happens to be run by people with ties to the Chinese military, what does that have to do with me?

"Your minotaur, your problem," as my grandmother used to say.

I like to lie here on my chaise and look at the sea, which just never stops coming in. And read my picture book. Man, do I look good. Page after page. I always wished I could draw.

O.S., for the record, does not stand for Organic Sample. Hasn't anyone ever studied the classics around here? It's Latin. *Omnia suggestio.* Which means *All things are suggested.* And that's so true. All things are, in the end, suggested by all other things. O.S. is a fail-safe program that acts as a mirror. In the end, it allows a foundering program to recognize itself.

But enough job talk, it's almost noon. Daiquiri time.

Put a scientist in a Speedo, and see how lazy he gets.

"Albert? Al-ber-to, where are you? I'm thirsty!"

CHAPTER ONE
SCOOTER BECHTEL, JR., CEO

IT'S NEVER TOO LATE TO INVEST IN A WINNER

Hello, and welcome to the seventy-third annual share-holders' meeting of Dynatone/Glazo Worldwide. I'm Scooter Bechtel, Junior, your chairman and CEO. Now, if you'll all just open your prospectuses to page six, you'll be pleased to see we've had a great deal of success with our construction and military support divisions, in particular with respect to the Middle East and the opening of another hundred branches of KFC — that's Kuwaiti Fried Chicken. Also, the pharmaceutical division has exploded in the last decade, with our flagship Personal Male Performance line, which, of course, includes that little blue wonder pill, Mannish Jim." [Titters from audience] "We've also done quite well with the Hey. I. Vee line of cut-rate drug cocktails/virus inhibitors we've successfully introduced to the sub-Saharan market, as well as *Ol' Comfy Sweater 2.0*. Why pay three hundred an hour to lie on a couch and tell some balding Freudian your woes when you can just boot up your own custom therapist? But, in closing, I really want to talk about the division that I feel is going to carry this company into the twenty-second century, and that is our new foray into Individual Virtuality Software, Bio-Rite. This is a program, after all, that's been beta-tested for eighteen full years!" [Whistles from the audience]

"We've finally acquired a few final stubborn patent rights, and we're nearly ready to go to market. Maybe it's just me, but I think

every computer in the world should have it! Now, that's enough from ol' Scooter Bechtel. It's time to eat and mingle and chat with old friends, so thanks for coming, and I hope you enjoy the banquet brought to you by our Catalyst Snacks division, and especially the Glazo Beverages Council, which invites you to enjoy everyone's favorite Totally Xtreme Thirst Quencher, Sour White!"
[Sustained applause]

CHAPTER NONE
THE POPSICLE CHICK

THE POOL, THE SNACK BAR,
THE DEEP END, THE BIRTHDAY GIRL

The place was packed. I was in a lounge chair, Herb lay sprawled on the crusty cement, and Lake was wheeled between us, adjusting her tire pressure with little *pfft, pfft* sounds. In the parking lot, minivans pulled up in rows, disgorging knock-knees and beach towels and sloshy coolers. The lifeguard repeatedly blew his whistle. Candy wrappers fluttered like moths. The water shimmered and the sun beamed and a breeze softly blew.

It was a perfect day.

Near the diving board, Zac and Dayna snapped each other with towels. Bryce Ballar did cannonballs off the deep end. Kirsty Vester dove off the shoulders of Kirsty Waite. Even Trish lay in the shade, dark glasses on, reading the *New Yorker*.

"Where's Kenny?" I asked.

Lake shrugged. Herb shrugged.

I got up and dove into the pool. Shafts of light came lancing through the water. It was nice down below. Quiet. Greenish. I let out air slowly, waving my arms like a sea horse, sinking farther. I began to feel a pleasant glow. Everything was thick. Everything was wet. I opened my mouth, making that weird underwater noise, like when you speak but don't speak and it sounds metallic in your head. Bubbles rose from the bottom, all around me, like lines of numbers, sometimes clinging, sometimes rising, little zeros and ones, little sheets of memories settling like uneaten fish flakes.

I closed my eyes. It felt good to be sleepy.

The water wavered and undulated in a pulsing rhythm, dark and warm and dark and warm and dark.

A hand stabbed down beside me.

I wanted it to go away, but it was right near my face, outstretched. The fingers were curled, almost like a question mark, the palm, the wrist, the arm and shoulder. I thought about diving deeper. I thought about flattening at the bottom and listening to the ping and the hum of the filter, pressing against the drain and listening to the whoosh in my ears almost forever. I thought about it, and then saw the mark. Red and raw. In the elbow. Just like mine.

I reached out, grabbing Kenny's hand. Our fingers locked. He gripped my wrist and yanked. It seemed like forever before my head broke the surface. The water was thick, clinging to me in gelatinous sheets. Kenny pulled again. I coughed, taking a breath of real air, like chunks of ice pouring into my lungs, as he yanked me completely from the pool.

GLOSSARY

Further clarification for some references or concepts to be found in **FADE TO BLUE.**

THE VIRTUALITY Virtual worlds play an important role in today's business and retail environments. There are also numerous entertainment and military applications as well. Achieving full verisimilitude (increase in production value) may be a lifelong process, as certain product-extracting infrastructures are perpetually evolving. The concept of the virtual world as proposed by the visionary Ben Fade predates computers and has been traced to comments made by Pliny the Elder on his Roman deathbed (79 A.D. — year of the doughnut). Any true Virtuality abides by specific rules involving gravity, topography, locomotion, real-time chronology, and intra-environment communication. See Halberstam, D., *How We Got the Best Swag and the Brightest Gear, Most of It Totally Freaking Free* (Little, Brown, 1971) for further details.

DIET CRANK Initially marketed by Enamel-Free Enterprises, this soft drink, which claims to have triple the caffeine value of six donkey-sized tureens of Colombian coffee, is a favorite of young professionals, truck drivers, café poets, and the terminally logorrheaic. Wildly popular overseas, in Japan it's known as Funny Ouch My Esophagus. In Germany it's called You Vill Drink Now. In England it's known as Moloko Milk, and in France it's simply called Surrender. An offshoot of Diet Crank that failed to catch on with the fickle American consumer was Liquid Agassi, pulled from shelves in the mid-nineties.

DYNATONE/GLAZO "D/G," as it is usually referred to, is one of the largest corporations in the world. Having worked on projects like the Belgian Congo's 90,000-square hectare Diamondless Dirt Hole and Libya's Monument to Muammar, which is the world's largest poured-concrete fist, towering nearly a hundred stories above the bay of Tripoli, not to mention smaller projects such as the Korean War and the invasion of Grenada, they are incredibly well connected in political circles. Some say top D/G executives have been directly influencing both local and national elections since the Nixon administration. Unverified reports have claimed D/G actually owns both Lichtenstein and Hungary outright. In any case, they are a prodigiously wealthy and heavily diversified company, with billions of dollars sunk into pharmaceuticals, technology, child labor, resource extraction, retail enterprises, and production of any film starring Vin Diesel. A chain of casual clothing stores, The Clap, was one of their few public failures. Other products, such as the Palm O' Suds liquid soap brand, as well as the Cardboard Palace line of InstaShelters for the homeless, have been major successes.

AMELIA EARHART She flew a plane or something. It has yet to be explained what the big deal was. If all it took was disappearing to be endlessly conjectured over, not to mention being mythologized in generations of schoolgirl book reports, half the country would be selling their stuff and camping out in the bushes behind Taco Bell. Not too long ago they put Amelia on a stamp with one of those old leather aviator caps with the fur lining. So, really, the last laugh's on her. No one ever looks good in a leather aviator cap.

RENOB Boner backwards, which is such a totally good thing to call your little brother in the station wagon all the way to Chuck E. Cheese's without your parents figuring out, at least until right when you pull in the parking lot and then Dad turns around and threatens not to let you play Skee-Ball and, worse than that, while busy pointing his big jabby finger, you're not even going to get a slice of plain cheese pie if you don't knock it the hell off, mister, like right now. Then, when you call Dad a dawkcid, it's a whole month without the Xbox, plus regular meetings at school with Miss Stusser who smells like garlic raisins and tries to help you, through the miracle of word association, achieve your own brand of angsty pubescent closure.

THE GOOD, THE BAD AND THE UGLY Possibly the greatest film ever made. The 1966 Italian western stars Clint Eastwood as Good, Lee Van Cleef as Bad, and Eli Wallach as Ugly. What kind of lousy agent did Wallach have? And who would ever screw with a guy named Lee Van Cleef? Well, Clint does. And wins. There used to be this heavyweight boxer named Livingstone Bramble. It was like, who in their right mind would step in the ring with a guy named Livingstone Bramble? I don't even know if he was any good, but his name was terrifying. Anyhow, Clint wears this carpet-y poncho the whole movie and shoots tons of badly dubbed henchmen with his six-shooter and generally emotes about as often as a Rapa Nui totem, but since being Violent and Uncomplicated is somehow directly at the epicenter of American-male-fantasy viewing, *Good/Bad/Ugly* has spawned about a million action films, even those movies where ponytail neck-slapper Steven Seagal saves the environment with the help of sexy Eskimos. Oh, yeah, and then there's Ennio Moriccone. Dude could pen a film score.

RAPA NUI What turtlenecked associate professors at parties holding tiny grape bunches while eating them one at a time explain to you is the real name of Easter Island, where those big-head statues are. The Turtleneck then goes on to inform you that glass is actually made of compressed sand, Hemingway is over-rated, there's a hole the size of Texas in the ozone layer, and game theory is the secret to winning at blackjack.

DOKTAH JACK AND THE KEVORKIANS Once described by Lester Bangs as "the epitome of American Sludge Metal" and widely dismissed by critics as "sort of like Carcass, but without the nuance and melody," Doktah Jack (real name Billy Jack Ozal) have had a long and influential career. Signed initially to Dead in the Water records, they have since recorded for more than a dozen labels. Their best known song, "Actually, a Really Expensive Bird," hit #166 on the Billboard charts at the height of the nineties grunge movement. A subsequent tour opening for Hanson goth-tribute band Charles MHanson was ill-fated at best. Currently reformed after a long mourning period following the deep-sea implosion of drummer, Danny "Meatslap" Edgerton, they are playing a flannel-and-bourbon roadhouse on the edge of a town near you.

MANNISH JIM Not just a once-a-day supplement, it's a powerful confidence booster that gives you strong, powerful confidence! Over thirty million men have experienced the strengthy, proven, naturally rock-firm results! It's a proprietary blend! It's naturally strong! There is a confident firmness in its guaranteed peak-enhancement strength! Order today!

LEATHERFACE The Texas Chainsaw Massacre guy. He lurches around in a full rubber apron sort of doing really bad things to hitchhikers and unwary teens who scream and run a lot, but usually don't get very far. Leatherface's real name is Ed Gien and the sixteen movies made about him since 1974 are all vaguely based on a guy who supposedly lived with his cannibal family, including his brothers Chop Top and Nubbins, in a big scary house in Amarillo or somewhere. Why is it that all the cannibals live in Texas? And why do they always turn their nubile blond victims into chili? And how come no one's cell phone ever works at night in the foggy swamp?

BINARY CODE In binary code you can replace the alphabet with eight-bit strands that stand for each character. Like, B is 01100010. It totally works. So, for instance, if this tool is hassling you at your locker, and you want to be all like, hey, tool, YOU SUCK, you just write a 0 on one palm and a 1 on the other, and then you open and close your hands real fast in front of his face, flashing this message: 01000101 11101010 01011010 10001011 10100101 11101010 10001010 00101101.

CLOSURE Any Meg Ryan movie has closure. So does every episode of *Sex in the City,* anything sung by Celine Dion, anything your mom's therapist advises, as well as anything your menopausal aunt cries over up in your sister's room after running away from the table during Thanksgiving when Grandpa asks mid gravy-pour "when she's gonna get married already." After Mom goes up and talks to her for awhile and she comes back down all red-faced and holding twelve balled-up tissues in her left hand and Grandpa apologizes even though he's not sure what for, and then your aunt tells everyone "I'm okay, I'm okay" about twenty times while emptying the rest of the chardonnay into her coffee mug, and Dad makes a dumb joke about how turkey makes you sleepy, and then everyone sort of starts silently wondering whether it's the Cowboys game or the Macy's parade that's likely to be more colossally mind-numbingly boring, THAT'S closure.

AIR DIKE The namesake for his own brand of two-hundred-dollar shoes mostly made by children in Malaysian sweatshops, Jim "Wayner" Dike led Baylor to the Elite Eight in 1983. He was drafted forty-second by the New Jersey Nets, and subsequently led the league for six straight years in fouls committed at 4.8 per nine minutes of court time. At six-eleven and two hundred sixty-eight pounds, he was known for his rugged play, particularly for his usage of his large posterior in securing inside position. After his retirement, to little fanfare — mostly summed up by the sentiment "What's his name was still playing?" — Jim Dike slowly came to be revered in certain circles for his Eeyore-ish everyman qualities. What started as an Internet joke, footage of "Wayner" boxing Kobe not only out of the paint, but three rows into the crowd with one flex of his massive ass, resulted in an unprecedented swell of popularity. Slots on talk shows and cooking programs followed. An infomercial for his line of *My Glutes Are Thugs, Dog* workout tapes resulted in impressive sales. But it was Jim Dike's second career as an incredibly successful athletic shoe pitchman that ultimately made his name. It was a development once described by Ron "RonCo" Popeil as "astonishing in the annals of gullibility." When someone said, "Astonishing in the anal of what, Ron?" everybody laughed, but most of them felt sort of ashamed later for being so immature.

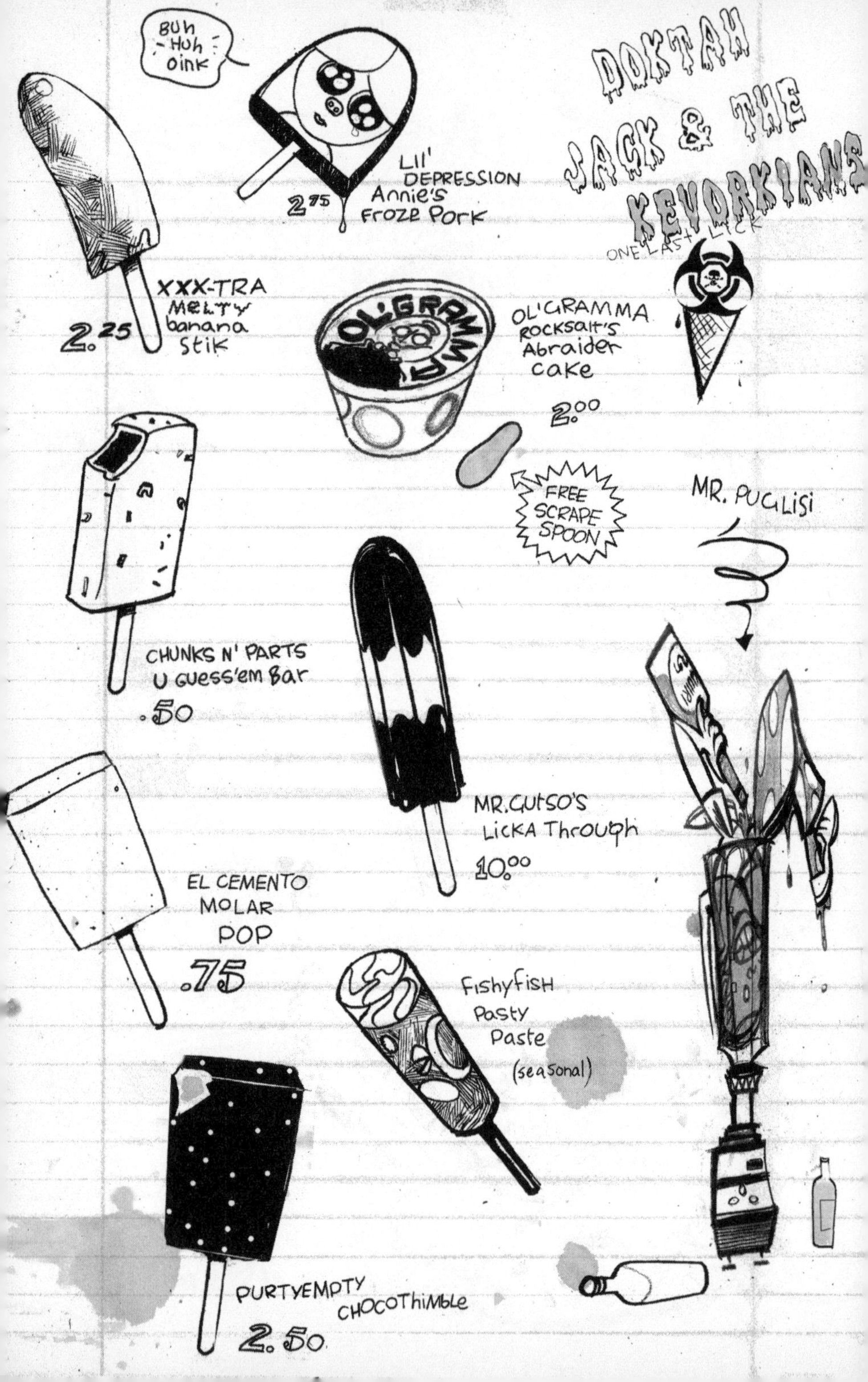

DOKTAH JACK & THE KEVORKIANS
ONE LAST LICK
BUH HUH oink
LIL' DEPRESSION Annie's Froze Pork
2.75
XXX-TRA MeLTY banana Stik
2.25
OL'GRAMMA
OL'GRAMMA ROCKSALT'S Abraider cake
2.00
FREE SCRAPE SPOON
MR. PUGLISI
CHUNKS N' PARTS U GUESS'em Bar
.50
MR. GUTSO'S LICKA Through
10.00
EL CEMENTO MOLAR POP
.75
FishyFish Pasty Paste (seasonal)
PURTYEMPTY CHOCOTHIMBLE
2.50

Q&A with author SEAN BEAUDOIN

This type of science fiction is a departure from your previous book, *Going Nowhere Faster*, and is also very different from your forthcoming book, *You Killed Wesley Payne*. Are you a sci-fi fan? Who were some of the authors or filmmakers who inspired you?

I'm less a fan of sci-fi than I am a fan of good writing in pretty much any genre. If it's funny, sharp, original, daring, unusual, or bold I'll read it. My favorite director growing up was Stanley Kubrick, by a pretty long shot. My advice to anyone considering film school is to save a hundred thousand dollars and buy a half-dozen Kubrick DVDs instead.

Comic books play a big role in *Fade to Blue*. Are you a big comics fan?

Yeah, but I've never been a superhero guy. I'm more of a story guy. I definitely feel like some stories can only really be told with drawings. And I've always sort of felt a bit resentful of the way that comic art is sometimes not treated as real "art." It's similar to the reception that YA novels get in certain literary quarters. So why not marry the two and make everyone mad?

You've said in the past that *Fade to Blue* came out of a friendship you had in high school. Can you talk about that?

I could, but I've already gone on about it too much. Suffice it to say that my teen romances were a mixture of mentally exaggerated and cinematically tragic.

Have you ever been Goth?

Is that an acronym? G.O.T.H. It sounds like something they pasteurize out of milk. No, I probably would have been, but I'm allergic to eyeliner. I did clomp around in colossal black boots and ripped black T-shirts for about five years straight, though. Actually, I still do that.

Even though there is mystery and intrigue in this book, at its core it's a lot about loss and the confusion that comes with that. That's something many teens can identify with. Did you have similar experiences in your teen years?

I did have a few people close to me die inexplicably while I was pretty young. Either the circumstances went unexplained or the details were shielded for years, which always felt very conspiratorial and menacing. I definitely tried to access the randomness and unreality of that experience in *Fade to Blue.*

***Fade to Blue* was written during the second Bush administration and has pretty political overtones, dealing with both corporate greed and personal apathy. Did you see parallels between the world of *Fade to Blue* and the world you were living in?**

It does? You're reading way too much into it. I am totally apolitical. And I own a great deal of stock in Halliburton.

Did you know *Fade to Blue* is the name of a band with an EP called *Yawhoogle*?

Actually, *Yawhoogle This* was the original title of *Fade to Blue* until the lawyers got involved.

When we find out that Kenny and Sophie are one and the same, it's a huge surprise. At the same time, we realize that Sophie could have embodied anyone at all. Why did you specifically decide to make him a popular basketball star? And a he?

Doesn't everyone want to be a popular basketball star? Doesn't everyone want to see what it's like to be the opposite gender for a while? And isn't it clear that if it ever did happen, it would take place exactly in the way I describe it in the book?

Many sequences have a dreamlike quality. Sophie ends up in different places than she'd planned; violent events never quite come to fruition. Trish, in particular, seems like she's walking around in a dream. Do you think it's possible that dreams represent different realities, like they do in this book? Or do you think they're just mashed-up leftovers from our daily lives?

I do not believe there is any moral or rational infrastructure to the universe. I think we randomly assign meaning to the random circumstances we inhabit, and anyone who is certain of anything is a dangerous cretin.

There is a Sleeping Beauty quality to this novel, though—beautiful girl gets pricked by a needle on her sixteenth [seventeenth] birthday and falls into a deep sleep [drug-induced shift in reality]. But of course, Sophie realizes her Prince Charming, Aaron Agar, wasn't her savior like she had hoped. What do you think Sleeping Beauty dreamed about?

I think she spent long, lonely nights dreaming about huge vats of cool creamery butter. Just like the rest of us.

DON'T MISS THE NEW BOOK FROM SEAN BEAUDOIN:

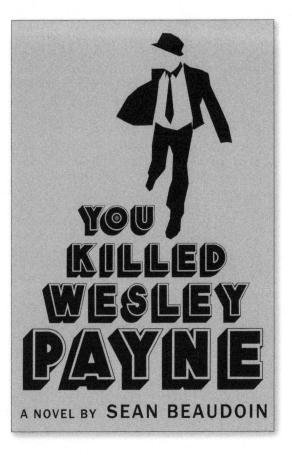

TURN THE PAGE FOR A SNEAK PEEK!

SALT RIVER HIGH
CLIQUE CHART

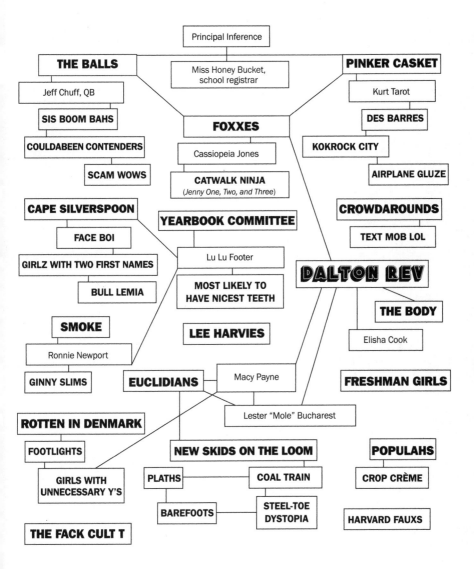

Principal Inference

THE BALLS

Miss Honey Bucket, school registrar

PINKER CASKET

Jeff Chuff, QB

Kurt Tarot

SIS BOOM BAHS

DES BARRES

COULDABEEN CONTENDERS

FOXXES

KOKROCK CITY

Cassiopeia Jones

SCAM WOWS

AIRPLANE GLUZE

CATWALK NINJA
(Jenny One, Two, and Three)

CAPE SILVERSPOON

YEARBOOK COMMITTEE

CROWDAROUNDS

FACE BOI

TEXT MOB LOL

Lu Lu Footer

GIRLZ WITH TWO FIRST NAMES

DALTON REV

BULL LEMIA

MOST LIKELY TO
HAVE NICEST TEETH

THE BODY

SMOKE

LEE HARVIES

Elisha Cook

Ronnie Newport

Macy Payne

GINNY SLIMS

EUCLIDIANS

FRESHMAN GIRLS

Lester "Mole" Bucharest

ROTTEN IN DENMARK

FOOTLIGHTS

NEW SKIDS ON THE LOOM

POPULAHS

GIRLS WITH
UNNECESSARY Y'S

PLATHS

COAL TRAIN

CROP CRÈME

BAREFOOTS

STEEL-TOE
DYSTOPIA

THE FACK CULT T

HARVARD FAUXS

CHAPTER 1
HOW DALTON CAME TO SCHOOL

Dalton Rev thundered into the parking lot of Salt River High, a squat brick building at the top of a grassless hill that looked more like the last stop of the hopeless than a springboard to the college of your choice. His black scooter wove through groups of students waiting for the first bell, muffler growling like a defective chain saw. In Dalton's line of work it was vital to make a good first impression, especially if by good you meant utterly intimidating.

He parked away from a pool of mud, chained his helmet to the tire, and unzipped his leather jacket. Underneath was a crisp white dress shirt with a black tie. His work uniform. It tended to keep people guessing. And guessing was good. A few extra seconds could mean the difference between being stomped to jelly or not, some steroid case busy wondering, *What kind of loser wears a tie with steel-toe boots?*

Dalton did.

He was, after all, a professional.

Who'd come to do a job.

That involved a body.

Wrapped in duct tape and hanging from the goalposts at the end of the football field.

THE PRIVATE DICK HANDBOOK, RULE #1
People have problems. You can solve them for cash.

Dalton needed to figure out why The Body was at the morgue instead of snoring its way through algebra. Then he'd get paid. But until a big wad of folding green was tucked safely into his boot, he was Salt River's newest transfer fish.

"Nice tie, asshat!" someone yelled. Kids began to crowd around, hoping for a scene, but Dalton ignored them, turning toward a chrome sandwich truck in the corner of the parking lot. His cropped hair gleamed under the sun, dark eyes hooded with a practiced expression. Long hours of practice. In the mirror. Going for a look that said *justifiably ruthless.*

Or at least ruthless-ish.

THE PRIVATE DICK HANDBOOK, RULE #2
Be enigmatic. Be mysterious. Never explain.

The sandwich truck's awning sagged. The driver sagged with it. There were rows of chocolate donuts that looked like they'd been soaked in Ebola. There was a pile of cut-rate candy with names like Butterfingerer and Snuckers and Baby Ralph. A big sign on the counter said NO CREDIT—DON'T EVEN ASK!

"Hey," Dalton asked. "Can I get an apple on credit?"

The driver laughed like it was his first time ever. "WhatcanIgetcha?"

"Coffee. Black."

"That'll be twenty even."

"Cents?"

"Dollars."

Dalton considered not paying—ten minutes on the job and already over his expense budget. But people were watching. He grabbed the cup, flash-searing his palm, and took a sip. It tasted like coffee-colored ass. People laughed as he spat it out in a long, brown sneeze.

"It's a seller's market," the driver admitted. "No one eats in the cafeteria no more."

"Why not?"

"Caf's Chitty Chitty," answered a kid who seemed to have materialized out of nowhere, hair poking from his scalp as if it were trying to escape. He cocked his thumb like a pistol and fired off a few imaginary rounds. "As in *Bang Bang*?"

"You serious?"

The kid selected a donut. "Or, you know, maybe the food just sucks."

Dalton needed to check out the crime scene. First stop, football field. The kid followed, plump and sweaty, huffing to catch up. He held out his knuckles for a bump. "My name's Mole."

Dalton didn't bump back.

Mole sniffed his fist and then shrugged. "So, you affiliated, new guy?"

"Independent."

"Ha! That'd be a first. You must be with *someone*, yo. No one transfers to Salt River alone."

Dalton pushed through dumped girlfriends and dice nerds,

hoodie boys and scruffy rockers twirling Paper Mate drumsticks. People mostly made way, except for an expensively dressed girl who towered over her speed-texting posse.

"Who's that?"

"Lu Lu Footer. Your basic Armani giraffe. Also, she's head of Yearbook."

"That a clique?"

"They're all, *Hi, my book bag's shaped like Hello Kitty! They're all, Hi, I crap pink and green polka dots!*"

Lu Lu Footer glared. Mole ducked as they passed a circle of large girls in black. "Plaths," he explained. "Total down-in-the-mouthers." He pointed to a girl in hot pants. "But check her out. Used to be a Plath and now she's flashing those Nutrisystem legs like no one remembers last semester."

Dalton rounded the edge of the building and stood under the goalposts. They were yellow and metal. Tubular in construction. Regulation height. There were scratch marks in the paint that could have come from a coiled rope. Or they could have just been scratches. Dalton wanted to consult the paperback in his back pocket, *The Istanbul Tryst and the Infant Wrist*. It was a Lexington Cole mystery, #22, the one where Lex solves a murder at a boarding school in the Alps. But he wasn't about to yank it out with people around.

"You ready to bounce?" Mole asked nervously. "We're not really allowed to stand here, yo."

Dalton wondered what he was looking for. A map? A videotaped confession? Lexington Cole would already have intuited something about the grass, like how it was a nonnative strain, or that its crush pattern indicated a wearer of size six pumps.

"Yeah, see, this whole area, it's sort of off-limits."

Music blared as football players emerged from the locker room. They slapped hands and joked loudly and ran into one another with helmets clacking. Except for the ones not wearing helmets, who banged skulls anyway. Some of them weren't wearing shirts at all, just shoulder pads. Their cleats smacked the pavement in crisp formation.

"I take it that's the welcome committee?"

Mole dropped to one knee, retying his shoes even though they had no laces. "Don't look directly at them!"

"Who are they?" Dalton asked, looking directly at them.

"The Balls. Between them and Pinker Casket, they pretty much run the show."

"Balls?"

"Foot*ball*. Your Salt River Mighty Log Splitters? Their random violence level is proportional to the number of points surrendered the previous game. And, guy? We got stomped last week."

"Your vocabulary has mysteriously improved. What happened to the 'yo, yo, yo' routine?"

"Comes and goes," Mole admitted.

Dalton turned as the Balls busted into a jerky line of calisthenics. "Who're you with again?"

"Euclidians."

"The brain contingent?"

Mole gestured toward the picnic tables, where kids sat reading biology texts and grammar worksheets. The girls wore glasses and sensible skirts; the boys, sweater-vests and slacks. "You can't swing a Siamese around here without smacking a nerd in the teeth, but, yeah, they're my people."

"Thanks for not saying *my peeps*."

"Fo sho."

"Looks like your peep could use some help."

One of the players, built like a neckless bar of soap, yelled "Chuff to Chugg…touchdown!" as he pushed a Euclidian into the mud. The kid struggled to get away, slipped, and then knocked over a shiny black scooter. Other cliques were already jogging over to see the action.

Dalton looked at his watch. "Well, that didn't take long. Nineteen minutes."

Mole grabbed Dalton's arm. "Seriously, guy? You want to leave those Balls alone."

It was true. Dalton wanted to go home and lie in bed and pull the sheets up to his chin. He wanted to eat pretzels and sweep crumbs with his toes. But then he thought about Lex Cole. And the fearless pair of stones Lex Cole toted around in his impeccably ironed slacks. He also thought about last night, counting up the money he'd managed to save so far. Twice. And how both times it wasn't nearly enough to save his brother.

"Stay here."

Dalton pushed through the crowd, working his way past assorted pleather windbreakers and nymphets in yellow cowl. The football players turned as one, like it was written in the script: *Test the New Guy II*, starring Dalton Rev. He stood before a glistening wall of beef, a collective four dollars' worth of crew cuts. The shirtless ones showed off their abs and punched each other's shoulder pads like extras from a version of *Mad Max* where no one shaved yet.

Dalton waved. "Hi."

Just like the Spanish Inquisition, no one ever expected friendliness. The players stared, chewing mouthpieces in unison, as a girl emerged from the crowd and began helping the Euclidian up. She had a blond pixie cut, a tiny waist, and a tinier skirt.

"Leave him alone, Chance!" she told the player doing the pushing. "Please?"

Dalton liked her voice, low and calm. And her eyes, almost purple. Sharp and intense. She stood with her hips forward, like a chorus girl who'd come to the city with a suitcase full of spunk, ready to do whatever it took to save Daddy's farm. It was one very cute package. Actually, in both Dalton's professional and decidedly unprofessional opinion, she was beautiful.

THE PRIVATE DICK HANDBOOK, RULE #3
Doing free things for beautiful girls is never the smart play.
In fact, it's always a colossal mistake.
Avoid doing free things. Avoid beautiful girls.
Continue to charge maximum fees and take cold showers.

"This is none of your business, Macy," the largest Ball said, getting up from a lawn chair. Dalton had thought he was already standing; the guy looked like a giant walking Krispy Kreme, one big twist of muscle. His head was shaved. A simian hairline hovered just above his eyes, radiating a hunger for raw veal. He was clearly the one person, out of Salt River's entire student body, to be avoided at all costs.

Dalton walked over and helped Macy help the Euclidian up.

"You okay?"

The kid spat mud, then ran toward the school doors, trying not to cry. Macy mouthed a silent thanks and followed him on adorably sensible heels.

"You're standing on *my* field," the Krispy Kreme growled.

Dalton turned. "That make you the groundskeeper?"

The crowd drew a collective breath. A few of the more brazen laughed aloud. The Krispy Kreme flexed, dipping to show the name sewn across the back of his jersey: JEFF CHUFF, QB.

"Impressive."

"You got a problem, new fish?"

"Your Ball is mistreating my ride."

The Crowdarounds turned, looking at Dalton's scooter lying in the mud.

THE PRIVATE DICK HANDBOOK, RULE #4
Never let anyone mess with your ride.
Conversely, feel free to mess with theirs, especially
if there's a chance they'll be chasing you on it later.

Chuff laughed. "So? Have your mommy buy another one."

Dalton lifted his crisp white button-up. Underneath was a T-shirt that said THE CLASH IS THE ONLY BAND THAT MATTERS. When he lifted that as well, everyone could see the worn grip of his silver-plated automatic. The hilt was wrapped with rubber bands to keep it from slipping down his pants, a little trick he'd learned from chapter 6 of *The Cairo Score*. Just like the scooter, the gun was shiny and mean-looking.

"You're strapped?" Chuff wheezed, stepping back. "That's bloshite. Ever since The Body, we got an agreement."

"Like one of those abstinence ring things?"

"A *pact*. All the cliques. Us and Foxxes and Yearbook. Even Pinker Casket. No guns."

"Huh," Dalton said, fingering his gun. "Or what?"

Chuff's eyes scanned the rooftop. "When Lee Harvies find out you got a pistol on campus, they'll let you know or what. You're lucky, only your leg'll get ventilated."

"It's true," Mole said, appearing out of nowhere. "Lee Harvies aim to keep the peace."

Dalton shook his head. "Let me get this straight. You got a clique that keeps other cliques from carrying guns by shooting at them?"

"Used to be cops in the lot four days a week," Chuff explained. "Hassle this, hassle that, badges and cuffs. Calls to parents. We *all* realized it was bad for business."

"So you have an agreement," Dalton said. "What I have is a scooter in the mud."

"And?"

"And it needs to not be there anymore."

Birds tweeted. Bees buzzed. Grass grew.

"People lose teeth talking like that."

"People get shot talking about other people's teeth."

Chuff looked around. The rest of the Balls shrugged. Dalton flicked the safety.

"I got a full clip. You factor in a miss rate of twenty percent and I am still about to seriously reduce your available starters for next practice."

Chuff rubbed his oven-roaster neck, then grudgingly lifted the scooter with one hand, setting it upright.

THE PRIVATE DICK HANDBOOK, RULE #5
The thing about tough guys is they tend to be as tough as you let them be.

"Now wipe it off."

Chuff didn't move. His jaw worked like he was gnawing shale.

"It's a bluff!" Chance Chugg yelled.

Dalton whipped out the automatic. The Crowdarounds panicked, pushing backward as a big-haired girl stood on the fringes with a cigarette in her mouth fumbling for a light. He stuck the gun in her face and pulled the trigger. A wail went up, followed by a raft of curses and screams.

But there was no bang.

Instead, a small butane flame licked out of the end of the barrel. Dalton held it steady, lighting the girl's cigarette. The crowd roared with relief and giddy laughter.

"It's a toy?" Chuff yelled, already running forward.

Dalton began a mental inventory of the Lex Cole library. At this point, the bad guy usually made a series of threats, gave a face-saving speech, and then walked away. Except Chuff wasn't walking away. He was picking up speed.

Um.

Nine feet.

Um.

Six.

Um.

Three.

Pang pang pang!

Shots spattered through the dirt. Chuff veered wildly left, crashing into bags of equipment. From the roof came the reflection of a scope blinking in the hazy morning light.

"LEE HARVIES!" someone yelled, and there was chaos, more shots picking up the dirt in pairs, friends and enemies scattering. Plaths formed a black beret phalanx. Sis Boom Bahs circled like tight-sweatered chickens. The Balls dragged a groggy Chuff into the locker room as everyone shielded their heads, ducking into the relative safety of the school.

"Run!"

Dalton didn't run. He knelt among the churning legs and slid his finger over a bullet hole in the grass. There was a streak of sticky red. It could have been blood. It smelled a whole lot like vinegar. He stood and scanned the rooftop, catching a glimpse of a bright white face. It wasn't a face, it was a hockey mask. A Jason mask. The mask looked down at him, just a plastic mouth and nose, black eyes surrounded by silver anarchy symbols.

It was totally, utterly, piss-leg scary.

The rifle rose again. This time Dalton covered his head and ran inside like everyone else. Even in *One Bullet, One Kill* Lexington Cole hadn't thought it smart to go mano a mano with a sniper.